Dumani Mandela

Young and on the run from Apartheid

© Dumani Mandela 2021

Young and on the run from Apartheid

Published by www.myminimalist.co.za

Hyde Park, Johannesburg, South Africa
dumani.mandela@icloud.com

ISBN 978-0-620-92666-9
eISBN 978-0-620-92667-6

2 4 6 8 0 9 7 5 3 1

All rights reserved. No part of this publication may be reproduced, stored in a retrieval system, or transmitted in any form by any means electronic, mechanical, photocopying, recording or otherwise without the written permission of the copyright owner.

Layout and publication facilitation by Boutique Books
Printed in South Africa by Digital Action

DEDICATION

I dedicate this book to my grandmother Evelyn and my grandfather Rolihlahla. Thank you for your principled pragmatism and open spirit. May you rest in eternal peace, and may your memory live on in my children, Iman and Micah.

Sandile walked slowly and sombrely through the local park on his way to school, carefully looking for warm cow dung to pack into the plastic bag in his hand. Thoughts of his great love ran through his mind. He thought how he would present the bag of cow dung to the love of his life Anelisa when he got to school. He had been in love with her since he could remember. He was ten years old and for all of his life that he could recall he had been in a love with Anelisa. She had moved into one of his grandmother's flats in the back of her house by the garage when they were three years old.

His grandmother Rhundu was a local businesswoman in the town of Cofimvaba. She was deeply religious and had an immeasurable social conscience. She was hard-working and honest to a fault. When Sandile was three years old, she had used the revenue from her spaza shop to build some flats in the back of her property for low-income people who could not afford their own housing in the town of Cofimvaba. Anelisa's family was the beneficiary of Rhundu's religious zeal and efforts to make the world she lived in more egalitarian for all.

He and Anelisa played together every day after school – sometimes marbles and sometimes a stick game that had been invented by the local kids from the nearby village of Emcumgcu. They both attended the primary school in Cofimvaba called Village. Except on Friday mornings, they would walk to school together through the local park to Village School, which was about five minutes from their home.

On Fridays, Sandile would get up at five and go to the local park, where some of the cows grazed, looking for warm cow dung. The cow dung was used to clean and maintain the floors in the school's classrooms. The boys would gather warm cow dung in the mornings, and it was the girls' responsibility to apply the cow dung to the classroom floors during their lunch breaks.

Sandile's mother and father were separated by their work but he had learned all he needed to know about love from them. His mother was a social worker in East London and his father worked in the mines in Johannesburg as a shop steward. He did not know what a shop steward was, but he surmised that his father was union representative and was in charge of managing the people when they went on strikes in the mines. This was a regular occurrence since his father would often come home during the many strikes and tell Sandile that he was negotiating with the mine owners for his future, by guaranteeing himself and all the other men who worked in the mines a better life by negotiating for liveable salaries.

His mother's job as a social worker was easier to understand and he knew that, like his grandmother, she helped people in need. His mother Phumla was a staunch Catholic who was very religious but extremely open-minded when it came to the needs of her children Sandile and Nobuhlali, Sandile's older sister. Although she seldom made Nobuhlali and Sandile go to church with her, since she lived East London, she did insist that they had to know the bible. She asked that Rhundu their grandmother have daily bible study with them. They would read some verses from the bible chosen by Rhundu and then she would recite biblical stories to them every night before bed. She had made sure that they both memorised the Lord's Prayer and, every evening after their bible study, they would recite the Lord's prayer together.

Rhundu was a Methodist, but her religion and her daughter's Catholicism were not in conflict. Sandile and Nobuhlali's father Aggrey was a Catholic and therefore, when he'd married their mother Phumla before they were born, she converted from being a Methodist to being a Catholic. For Sandile it was all much of a muchness. Jesus was Jesus and God was God, Jesus' Father, and Mary was Jesus' mother.

He had difficulty, however, with the Holy Spirit since it was incorporeal and did not have human representation. For him, the closest thing he had seen which resembled the Holy Spirit was lightning during a thunderstorm. He was the kind of person who needed physical representation of everything in order to understand religion.

On many of his walks to school with Anelisa, he spent the time narrating to her the religious stories that his grandmother had told him and his sister the night before. His sister Nobuhlali did not attend Village but attended a nearby Catholic convent run by some nuns from surrounding villages. Their grandmother had witnessed so many young girls in the village of Cofimvaba getting pregnant that she thought it was best to shield Nobuhlali from this phenomenon by sending her to the local Catholic convent.

Since Anelisa did not have the privilege of going to the convent, Sandile thought that, in his daily narrations of his biblical stories to Anelisa, he could also impart to her some of his spiritual wealth. In some way he hoped that this would shield her from any harm that would befall her in life. He wanted to protect her and for her to feel safe in his presence, as his mother felt protected and safe with his father.

2

"Good morning, nkwenkwe." This was a name Sandile had come to hate because every time someone called him inkwenkwe it was a reminder that he was not a man and that he still had a long way to go before he could be with Anelisa as his girlfriend. He was still a boy and uncircumcised [inkwenkwe]. Sandile was late for school again for the umpteenth time and he was going to get another beating from the teacher that he loathed the most, Mrs. Nontish.

Mrs. Nontish was rather sadistic about the corporal punishment that she gave out to students who came into school late. She would ask them to stick out their hands with their palms facing downward and then she would take the edge of the ruler and hit them several times on the top part of their hand. Sandile tried in vain to explain to Mrs. Nontish that he was late because he could not find cow dung, but his pleas fell on deft ears.

"Mam Nontish, excuse my tardiness but I could not find fresh cow dung. I had to walk behind the cows in the park for two hours, waiting for them to poo so that I could collect the cow dung." He wanted to tell her exactly why he was late, but he also did not want to beg since Anelisa was looking at him from the corner of the classroom.

"So why did you not wake up earlier, Sandile? You knew you had to bring fresh cow dung today since it is Friday. You have delayed your whole class. Class, what do you think I should do?"

All the children wanted to see Sandile squirm just a tad, since every year since the children were in Sub A he'd come at the top of his class as the number one student. They were now in Standard 3 and Sandile continued to outperform the other students in class.

"Everyone who thinks Sandile should get a hiding for being late, raise your hand."

All of the children raised their hands except for Anelisa, who simply put her hands over her mouth as if anticipating the pain for Sandile. Sandile could not control his annoyance and blurted out, "Bloody heathens! This class is full of opinions."

"Nkwenkwe, what are you saying now? Do you want a double beating for your foul tongue? Are you implying that the students are overly opinionated because their consensus is for you to rightfully receive punishment for being late?"

"Kind of, Mrs. Nontish, but as my mother always says – opinions are like arseholes. Everyone has one, so please do your worst."

Sandile closed his eyes and stuck out his hand and prepared for the ruler to make contact with the back of his hand.

"Well done, nkwenkwe, you have just earned yourself another well-deserved trip to the principal's office and to get another sjambok beating yet again. But before you go, I must administer my own punishment for your tardiness."

Mrs. Nontish took out her wooden ruler and struck Sandile ten times on the back of his hand, one lash for every minute that he was late for class. Sandile kept in the tears from the throbbing pain, not wanting to seem less of a man in front of the class, and especially not in front of Anelisa.

Anelisa still had her hands over her mouth and Sandile could see tears flowing from her eyes. As always, she felt the pain for his punishment as she had on so many occasions. He could not tell if she was crying because of the beating he had just received from Mrs. Nontish or for the one he was going to receive from the principal. She reluctantly raised her hand to get Mrs. Nontish's attention.

"Mam, but he told you that he had to wait on the cows for two hours. I don't understand why you had to do that."

There was an eerie silence in the class, with Mrs. Nontish staring at Anelisa, hoping she would be intimidated, turn away at some point and recant her words. But Anelisa did not back down. She stared straight back at Mrs. Nontish. Sandile was rubbing the back of his hand, trying to abate the pain, while mentally preparing for the beating that he would get at the hands of the principal and his sjambok.

"I just found that so unnecessary. And you knew that the class was not going to vote in Sandile's favour because they never do. Maybe you should stop giving him such high marks and he might make some friends."

"Young lady, I am not doing this for your entertainment or mine. I am doing this for Sandile's benefit. I am assisting him to become a responsible young man. It's not enough that he has good grades. He has to learn to be more responsible for his actions. And you are not here in my class to make friends, young lady, but to learn."

Anelisa was not going to back down.

"So why send him to the principal's office then, if you have taught him his lesson?"

"You know why, Anelisa: because of that devilish mouth. This child is bright but, dear God, his mouth is of the devil. He is going to the principal's office and that is that!"

There were no further words between Mrs. Nontish and Anelisa, just a staring contest to see who would back down first. Sandile did not want Anelisa to be sent to the principal's office as well and chose to defuse the situation.

"Well, I guess that is my cue to go to the principal's office then."

The whole class let out mellow laughter, knowing how intense Anelisa's loyalty was to Sandile. She had a deep love that the children in her class had come to understand in her intensity for her feelings for Sandile and she always sought to protect him from harm from others and himself.

Mrs. Nontish took her eyes off Anelisa and took a seat behind her desk. Anelisa was the one student who could intimidate Mrs. Nontish, not only because she was a good student – she always came in second in her class, closely behind Sandile – but also because she was loyal to Sandile to a fault. Mrs. Nontish thought that Sandile and Anelisa behaved and acted more like husband and wife than many married couples that she had observed. In the year of teaching Sandile and Anelisa, she and the students had come to harbour a secret respect for their love for one another.

Mrs. Nontish began to organise the papers on her desk in preparation for the mathematics lesson of the day. She always started off the day with math and ended with English, since she found as the day progressed the children lost interest in their lessons. Her position was that the children could always learn English outside the classroom whilst watching television or practising with one another, but math had to be taught in the classroom.

"Alright, Sandile, please go to the principal's office. I am sure you will sweet-talk him as you always do and find a way to escape your punishment."

Sandile glanced lovingly at Anelisa, as if to thank her for her intervention. He was not scared to go and see the principal Mr. Dabula. Mr. Dabula was a short, soft-spoken man, who only administered corporal to his students as a last resort. He preferred to talk his students through any problems that emerged during their studies. He took a special interest in Sandile because of his performance in school and also because of his sharp wit.

He had at first thought that Sandile's relationship with Anelisa would slow down Sandile's school performance and personal growth. However, after watching them for a number of years and seeing how they supported and motivated one another, he'd also developed a secret respect for the children.

Mr. Dabula used the times that Sandile was sent to his office as a chance for him to develop Sandile's interpersonal skills and to introduce him to the art of morning tea. As Sandile approached the door to Mr. Dabula's office, he tried to think of the perfect opening line to a conversation with Mr. Dabula. Mr. Dabula appreciated happy and grounded children and would not discipline them if the child immediately showed remorse for their actions. Sandile knew he had one sentence to make an impression on Mr. Dabula. He knocked on the door softly twice, in case Mr. Dabula was in a bad mood and did not want to be bothered. He would be able to tell what he should say based on the way Mr. Dabula answered the knock.

"Nkwenkwe, is that you again? Dear God, you are coming to my office every Friday now?"

Sandile slowly opened the door to give Mr. Dabula time to open up to the idea that he might not need corporal punishment this time around. He stuck his head through the small opening of the door.

"Yes, it's me, Master Dabula. Mind if I join you for tea?"

Mr. Dabula let out a bellowing laugh, knowing that he would not have to administer punishment to Sandile today since he'd shown some remorse and his quick wit yet again.

"Sure, Nkwenkwe. Come in and take a seat."

Mr. Dabula's office was a small room in the middle of the two long parallel face brick buildings that constituted the Village School. In the centre, between the buildings, were the morning registration grounds where student's names were called out in the morning. Mr. Dabula's office sat at the back of the school, behind the registration areas in between the parallel buildings, next to the teachers' lounge. He could see every classroom from his office window and had a clear view of the whole school.

"Nkwenkwe, you know I can see everything from this office, and I noticed that you walked in ten minutes late to class this morning."

Sandile snapped back. "Sir it was not my intention, but the cows would not poo, and I had to walk behind them this morning for two hours in the park waiting for them to poo so I could collect fresh cow dung for the class floor."

"Nkwenkwe, I can't tell if your obsession with fresh cow dung is a result of your concern for your class floor, or if it's to make Anelisa's job easier than the other girls', who might receive hard cow dung from the other boys when they have to clean the floors."

Sandile looked down and fiddled with his fingers and could not tell if he should be on the defensive with Mr. Dabula or should stay calm. He decided to opt for respect in order to pacify Mr. Dabula.

"Master Dabula, I like to do things correctly and properly. Like yourself, I like perfection, whether it's for myself or for Anelisa, since she is like a sister to me."

"Nkwenkwe, you already have a sister and I highly doubt you think of Anelisa as your sister."

It became increasingly clear that Mr. Dabula did not want to administer punishment to Sandile and he decided to take a more relaxed tone with him.

"Sir, one day she will be my wife!"

"Well, you already behave like husband and wife. All you need now are the rings and the wedding ceremony."

Sandile was confused, as he did not know exactly what husband and wife acted like, except from the example of his father and his mother, who had a loving relationship, although they lived so far apart. Sandile's father Aggrey was from Accra, Ghana, and also used to be a teacher in village. But he thought his services were needed elsewhere in South Africa and so he had gone to live in Johannesburg to be a shop steward and work with trade unions. He spent a lot of time educating his fellow employees on how to exercise their rights and also lobby for better work conditions.

He enjoyed his work and was a community leader in the village of Cofimvaba. He'd come to South Africa in 1972 and had met Sandile's mother Phumla a year later, in 1973 and soon after they had Nobuhlali in 1974 and Sandile two years later in 1976. The year now was July 1985 and a state of emergency had been declared in South Africa.

Mr. Dabula wanted to talk to Sandile about what this meant for his father's work. He also had other things on his mind like manhood and the meaning of love, but was not quite sure how he should structure the conversation with Sandile.

"You know, Sandile, we live in difficult times, and I am sorry that this will be the last time that we will speak for a while."

Sandile was confused and did not know how to respond to Mr. Dabula. Was he ill and was he going to die on that day?

"Sir, is everything okay?"

"You know, Sandile, going to the mountains to get circumcised does not make one a man. It is just a ritual that we have been going through for centuries so we pass it down from one generation to the next in hopes that we will also pass down lessons of manhood to the next generation."

Sandile wondered if this was it. Would Mr. Dabula put him in the back of his van and whisk him off to the mountains to get circumcised on this day? He was somewhat excited and at least hoped that now people would stop calling him inkwenkwe. But at the same time, he was fearful of the manhood cut. His initial thought was to delay Mr. Dabula as much as he could and then, when he was not paying attention, to run out of his office to his grandmother's house and tell her that Mr. Dabula wanted to take him for initiation at such a young age. His grandmother would certainly be furious, he thought.

"As I was saying, Sandile, I have learned a lot about manhood from you in the way you treat Anelisa and how she treats you. She is becoming a woman in developing her nurturing abilities."

Sandile took a deep breath. Perhaps Mr. Dabula was leading elsewhere with his conversation and he was not going to take him away to circumcision school.

"Sir, do I have to get married to Anelisa now? Should I not go to circumcision school first?"

Mr. Dabula laughed out loud, stood up from his desk and walked over to Sandile and hugged him. He looked down at him.

"Ideally, Sandile, in five years from now you would have gone to the mountains for initiation. I don't think, however, that you will get that chance as you have to leave here in the next hour when there is a window to take you to the airport in East London, where you will fly to Johannesburg and then from there to London. You will meet your father and your sister. Your grandmother applied for a passport for you already, and a US visa, and has packed your bags. They are in my car for me to take you to the airport in East London. Your mother is already in the United States of America. She left five months ago to get things ready for your family's arrival. Please, you must understand, Sandile, that we live in difficult times and that is why I must help you to leave."

"But what about Rhundu, my grandmother? I have to tell her I am going. I have to tell Anelisa where I am going."

Sandile was panic stricken. He still had so many things to do and experience in the village of Cofimvaba and could not bear leaving his village so abruptly. Mostly, he thought about all the moments he had planned to spend with Anelisa in his mind and could not reconcile leaving her behind.

'But, sir, I thought you were going to take me to the mountains to become a man so I can marry Anelisa. I don't want to go to America, I want to stay here and become a man and marry Anelisa."

"Sandile, there are too many complications with going to the mountains in our community at the moment. Many young men are dying due to infections because of circumcision doctors who are not well trained. It will be better for you to go to a hospital to become a man. You will achieve the same result in a safer environment. You can do all of this in America."

Sandile's panic turned into anger as he felt that Mr. Dabula was taking away his chance to become a man in his own village. He was destroying his rights of passage by making him go to this foreign place America which he had only seen on TV with shows like the A Team and MacGyver.

"Take me to the hospital now then, sir, so I can get circumcised and become a man, and then I can take my grandmother and Anelisa with me to America."

"That will not be possible, Sandile, as you have to leave for East London in the next half an hour when your travel window opens up. We have a border patrol that will give you safe passage from Transkei then."

"But why does my family have to leave to this place America? Why can we not stay here?"

"Things are complicated in South Africa at the moment, Sandile, and your parents will explain to you when you get to America. Please try to understand. I am sure the ancestors will forgive you for not going to the mountains for circumcision and going to a hospital in America."

"What do the ancestors have to do with this, sir? You are confusing me."

"You will understand when you are older, Sandile. For now, please, we must prepare you to leave here."

Sandile had so many unanswered questions and he wondered what Anelisa would think if he left without saying goodbye. She would feel abandoned by him and this would break their trust forever. He could not bear to let her down or break her heart. She had become his life and he derived his life meaning from the love he received from her. All he knew was that he could not leave her behind. Even though he was not yet a man, he wanted to take her with him.

"I want to speak to Anelisa right now, sir, please!"

"Alright, nkwenkwe, wait here in the office and I will go and get her in the classroom so that Mrs. Nontish does not ask any questions."

From the office, Sandile could see Mr. Dabula walking to his Standard 3 classroom. A minute later, he came out with Anelisa and was signalling her with his hand to hurry into his office. Anelisa looked confused and scared. She knew that something was wrong, although she did not fear being punished for any wrongdoing. As she walked to the office, she feared something might have happened to Sandile during his punishment and she thought the worst.

When Anelisa and Mr. Dabula walked into the office Sandile was sitting in the corner of the office in a foetal position, shaking. Anelisa began seething with uncontrollable anger.

"What have you done to him, Master Dabula?"

"Anelisa, no. Don't yell at him; he has done nothing. I have to leave here today, and I will not be back for a while."

"What, leave to where? Where are you going? And have you told Rhundu?"

Mr. Dabula intervened. "Nkwenkwe, we don't have much time. Please say goodbye to Anelisa and let us go."

"Anelisa, I have to go to meet my family in America. I promise I will come back for you when I am a man."

Anelisa knew from the expression of haste in Mr. Dabula's face that this would be the last time she would see Sandile for years to come. She hugged him with all her strength and did not let go. She was, however, confused as to where America was.

"Sandile, are you going to that place that we see on the A team and MacGyver? Is that America? Will I also see you on TV as well?"

Mr. Dabula thought it was best to take some time to explain to Anelisa and Sandile what was happening so that their goodbye could be more peaceful.

"Anelisa, you will not see him on TV. I was explaining to Sandile that we live in difficult times. As you both know, we live in this homeland called the Transkei and, as black people, we are somewhat prohibited by the laws from living in certain parts of South Africa and from pursuing political action for our equality within South Africa.

"Sandile's father works with the trade unions in Johannesburg and is very involved in our liberation movement and therefore has attracted the attention of the security police. He left the country last night with Sandile's sister Nobuhlali. Sandile's mother is also politically active as an underground operative in East London, using her job as a social worker as cover. Therefore, the security police were after her as well and she left for America five months ago.

"Rhundu, Sandile's grandmother, was afraid that the security police would come after Sandile as well, so she has asked that we organise for him to leave the country today. She did not want to tell Sandile before, in case the information about his departure came to the knowledge of some members of our community who are working with the security police. Anelisa, do you understand why Sandile has to leave now?"

Anelisa nodded her head, tears running down her face. She thought about her brother Solomozi, whom the security police had taken from her parent's house in the dead of night, and how traumatic the experience had been for her and her family. She had a flashback to the night that they'd dragged him through the house screaming and had beat him until he was unconscious and then put him into a security van. Five months later, her family received Solomzi's body and the security police told Anelisa's family that he had hanged himself. She could not bear to go through the same experience with Sandile.

She suddenly panicked when she realised the gravity of Sandile's situation and more tears streamed down her face. "Sandile, please, you must leave with Mr. Dabula now. I don't want what happened to my brother Solomozi to happen to you. Mr. Dabula, please take him now!"

Mr. Dabula hugged Anelisa and rubbed her back in an effort to calm her down. She started crying out loud and he was afraid other teachers in the school would hear her.

"Please, Anelisa, do not make too much noise. We do not know which teachers are also working with the security police here at Village. There is a lot of witchcraft in this small town and people are always being abducted for ominous reasons by the security police. I don't want them to come after your family again, as a result of an informant here at school."

Anelisa, understanding the sensitivity of the situation, stopped crying immediately and wiped the tears from her eyes. She was trying to put on a brave face for Sandile and also let him know she would be fine.

Sandile was desperate for more time with Anelisa and could not find the right words to say to her. "If I was a man now, I would take you with me to America. I promise I will come back when I am a man and deal with these security police who hurt your brother."

Mr. Dabula wanted to take some of the pressure of manhood off Sandile and to give Anelisa some hope for their future.

"Sandile, as I said to you before, you do not need to go to the mountain to be a man. You will be able to do it in hospital in America. I am sure the ancestors will forgive you and then, when you are ready, Anelisa will be here waiting for you."

"But, sir, if I don't go to the mountain, the other boys will call me inkwenkwe all my life. I must go."

"Sandile, manhood is not found in the mountain but is found in your heart and in how you treat others. God and the ancestors will see how you have treated Anelisa and will be kind to you, as they have granted you manhood now through your maturity. We live in difficult times and you must learn now at an early age to be able to make difficult choices. That is the essence of manhood."

"Sir, you said we had an hour. Can you not take me to the mountain now before we leave? I want to take Anelisa with me."

Anelisa could feel the love Sandile had for her pouring through his soul and his plea to Mr. Dabula. She grabbed his hand to comfort him and let him know that she would be fine. She avoided eye contact with him, knowing that if she were to look upon him, she would break down in tears again.

"No, Sandile, that will not be possible. We do not have the time, and your lift to the airport will be here shortly. I can tell you that going to the mountain has its own complications and when I went there in my youth I had difficulties and I ended up in hospital. The doctor who was performing my procedure was not well trained and I got an infection and had to be treated in hospital. Many young people are going to the hospital to become men nowadays and there is no shame in that."

Anelisa squeezed Sandile's hand in hers and, without looking at him in the eyes, she concurred with Mr. Dabula.

"Sandile, Mr. Dabula is right. It's better to go to the hospital and then you can come back from America when you are a man. I will be here in Cofimvaba waiting for you."

Sandile gave Anelisa another hug and, as he pulled away, there was a soft knock on the door. The person knocked three times and then waited ten seconds and knocked another three times and opened the door. In came a tall, burly white man in his mid-fifties. It was Mr. Andreas, who owned a local spaza store in town. Sandile and Anelisa grabbed one another in angst, not knowing what to expect. They thought perhaps he had come to inform on them to the security police.

Mr. Dabula shook Mr. Andreas' hand and they both looked down at the frightened children.

"Don't worry, nkwenkwe, Mr. Andreas is here to take you to East London. There will be fewer questions if the security police do a border check because they will think you are his errand boy. I will drive in the opposite direction to East London, to Queenstown, in order to somewhat misguide the security police in case we are being followed, whilst you and Mr. Andreas drive towards East London. Mr. Andreas is a friend of your grandmother Rhundu and has been assisting us to organise your departure during church."

There was so much subterfuge that Anelisa and Sandile had difficulty keeping up with what was taking place, but they both wanted to be strong for one another. Mr. Andreas addressed Sandile in a soft tone and in a baritone voice.

"Nkwenkwe, your grandmother has given me your bags and your passport to take you to East London. I will tell you what you must do to get to London to meet your father and sister on the way to the airport in East London. Come, we must go whilst our window is open for travel."

Sandile let go of Anelisa's hand and followed Mr. Andreas out of the office door. He looked back at Anelisa one more time and rushed over to her and gave her one more hug and a kiss on the cheek. The hug was to show her that he would miss her dearly and the kiss was to let her know that, when he was a man, he would return for her. His departure with

Mr. Andreas was quite abrupt, which left Anelisa with a hollow feeling in her heart.

"Come, Anelisa, we must make sure you get back to your classroom before questions are asked. If Mrs. Nontish asks you where Sandile is, tell her that I have sent him home to his grandmother Rhundu for his insolence."

Anelisa scurried out of Mr. Dabula's office and ran back to her classroom. When she entered the class, she was out of breath and was breathing deeply. Mrs. Nontish took notice.

"So, I guess you were also given punishment. Birds of a feather flock together. Where is Sandile?"

Without hesitating and with no emotion she answered, "Mr. Dabula sent him home for his insolence."

"Serves him right. That boy's mouth is of the devil."

Anelisa walked over to her seat in the corner in the back of the classroom. On her seat was a Pep plastic bag, which was still warm. It was the fresh cow dung that Sandile had got her that morning. It was the last reminder of the boy whom she had come to love. She was reminded of how meticulous he was about everything and also how he tried to make her life easier whenever he was around. She took the cow dung and placed it on the floor on the side of her seat. It was the last reminder of the boy she loved, who would one day come back a man.

That afternoon, she patiently waited outside the classroom with all of the other girls, water bucket in one hand and a plastic bag with cow dung in the other, whilst the boys removed the chairs and the desks from the classroom.

She thought about Sandile's future and what kind of man he would grow up to be.

When the time to clean the floors with the cow dung came, she rushed into the classroom to the place where Sandile's desk sat and she picked her spot to clean. She took some cow dung out of the plastic bag and applied it to the floor in semicircles whilst sprinkling some water on it to make sure it would absorb into the floor. As she went through her ritual, she said the Lord's Prayer and asked that the ancestors and God protect Sandile in his travels.

With each semicircle she was letting Sandile's spirit go and acknowledging the role he had played in her life by cleaning the area where his desk used to be. As she cleaned, the water in the cow dung mixed with her tears and she thought about all of the mornings that they had spent together, with him reciting biblical stories on their way to school. She thought about all the attention that he used to give her to make sure she felt safe and protected in his presence.

Mrs. Nontish noticed her crying as she cleaned with the cow dung on Sandile's space. "What's wrong now, ntobi? Sandile should appreciate you cleaning his space every Friday. When he comes back on Monday, he will thank you."

Anelisa knew that she had said her goodbyes and she would not see Sandile for years to come. "It's nothing Mrs. Nontish, I am just so grateful that Sandile took his time getting me this fresh cow dung since it made my cleaning easier."

"Yes, that boy is always so meticulous and is always thinking of you first. I am sure you are also always thinking of him as well."

For the next couple of years, that would be the extent of her and Sandile's relationship. He would remain in her thoughts and imagination, part of her longing for a time gone by. Nostalgia would become her friend and comfort her as she grew into a young woman. But that morning, she did not want to give anything about Sandile's departure away, and so she kept the façade going along with Mrs. Nontish.

"Yes, mam, I am sure I will see him on Monday when we come back to school."

Mrs. Nontish silently answered back. "Sometimes, child, I think the ancestors have ordained you to be together in this life!"

3

The ride to the airport with Mr. Andreas was a silent affair. Sandile could tell this was not the first time that Mr. Andreas had done something like this and he seemed rather calm for a man committing a crime against the state in assisting Sandile to get out of the country. Although the process was all legal, in how Sandile's grandmother had got him the passport and his American visa, the security police still wanted to find his parents for contravention of state statutes against supporting banned political organisations. Sandile being in the country when his parents had fled would be dangerous for his whole family and himself.

When they got to the town of Engcobo, Mr. Andreas finally spoke to Sandile. "We are going to stop at the BP gas station in Engcobo. Just try and act casual. I have to go to the rest room, but you don't have to get out of the car. If you look in the back seat, I have packed a cooler box with some snacks in it for you."

When they got to the BP gas station in Engcobo, Mr. Andreas casually got out of the car and spoke in isiXhosa to the petrol attendant to fill up the tank of his 4x4 Land Cruiser. The petrol attendant did not pay any attention to Sandile and simply thought he was the errand boy for the white man. Sandile reached to the rear seat, opened the cooler box, pulled out a sandwich and reluctantly took a bite. He was still unsure of Mr. Andreas and thought he could have been sent by the security police to turn him in whilst fooling his grandmother and Mr. Dabula. Perhaps the sandwich was poisoned.

He stopped eating it, looked at it for a moment and opened the car window to offer it to the petrol attendant. The petrol attendant thanked him but not before his actions had been observed by Mr. Andreas coming out of the toilet. Mr. Andreas knew he had a short time to gain Sandile's trust, as he did not want things to go wrong at the border control. Mr. Andreas paid the petrol attendant, thanked him in isiXhosa and slid into the driver's side of the car, not wanting to frighten Sandile with any sudden movements. He could tell the boy was scared and still confused about the events of the morning at his school.

They were both silent for another hour until they got to the city of Umtata. Mr. Andreas knew that it was another hour and a half to the Transkei border and he had to make Sandile comfortable.

"You know, nkwenkwe, this is the city where I first met your father Aggrey. We were both teachers in mathematics at the University of the Transkei in 1972 when he arrived from Accra, Ghana. That is also where he met your mother Phumla as well. Your father was never satisfied with how this country was and brought a lot of learning experiences from Ghana about national independence from colonial rule."

"Sir, what is colonial rule?"

"Nkwenkwe, it is when a foreign minority rule over the local majority by force."

Mr. Andreas thought he had lost Sandile in his explanation, but he was pleasantly surprised by his answer.

"Oh, you mean like when white people suppress the rights of black people in South Africa and Africa for material or resource gain. Reminds me of one of my father's history lessons he used to give my sister and me before bed when he would visit from Johannesburg."

"Mr. Dabula told me you always came number one in your classes. Perhaps I should stop referring to you as inkwenkwe."

"Don't worry, sir, it does not offend me as I am still not circumcised yet and I have to go to the mountains in five years when I turn fifteen or sixteen. Then I will go back to Cofimvaba and take Anelisa with me."

"Oh, I see. So, you are in love." Mr. Andreas broke out into light laughter.

Sandile was now a tad bit confused and wanted to explain himself. "Anelisa is like my sister and we have grown up together. I don't know how I will be able to cope without her. She always protects me and listens to my stories. I am like her brother."

"Well, I guess that is fine, kwedini [young man]. In the end, most married couples become like brother and sister in the depth of their love. People understand one another as family as time progresses, rather than as lovers. I guess you were lucky then to have known that kind of love."

Sandile had no answer for Mr. Andreas and stared at the road ahead. They did not speak again for their entire trip to East London airport. Mr. Andreas had succeeded in getting Sandile's trust and they were both comfortable with one another. They passed the border gate with no complications and arrived at East London Airport at five in the afternoon. Mr. Andreas dropped Sandile off in the domestic departures driveway.

"Just walk straight through the main doors and there will be someone to take you to your departure gate inside the main entrance."

"Who will take me, sir? I don't understand. You told me you were going to tell me how to get to Johannesburg and then London to meet my father and my sister."

"Sorry, young man, plans have changed and this is as far as I can go. I don't want to attract unnecessary attention to myself. If there are security police in the airport, they might think I am smuggling you out of the country."

Sandile begun to sob a bit but stopped the tears, as he wanted to act like a man in front of this stranger who had taken him hours from home and was now abandoning him at an airport far from his village of Cofimvaba. He looked around for a taxi. He knew how to take taxis, as he had often taken taxis by himself to visit his relatives in the surrounding villages to Cofimvaba.

"Sir, can I have some money for a taxi back to Cofimvaba, since you are going to leave me by myself here at this airport?

"Kwedini, don't worry. As Mr. Dabula told you, I am friends with your grandmother and you father, and I would not lead you astray. Trust me. Walk through the main entrance and there will be someone to help you to get to London to meet your father and sister."

Hesitantly, Sandile stepped out of the vehicle and walked to the back of the Land Cruiser to get his bags from Mr. Andreas.

"I guess this is it then, young man. God willing, I will meet you when you are a man in a couple of years. God bless your travels and be safe."

Before Sandile could respond, Mr. Andreas walked to the front of the car, quickly got into the driver's seat and sped off. Sandile was still a bit apprehensive and thought maybe if he caught a taxi his grandmother would be able to pay the driver when he got to Cofimvaba. He contemplated his next move until he got enough strength to walk through the main entrance of the airport.

On the other side of the entrance was a majestic sight – a person he'd thought he would not see for years to come. His grandmother Rhundu stretched out her arms and Sandile ran and hugged her as if it were the first time they had met.

"My brave little boy. I am sorry you had to experience what you had to go through today, but it is not safe for you in the country at the moment and you must go. We don't have much time."

She handed him his boarding tickets for the East London flight to Johannesburg and the Johannesburg to London flight.

"Just follow the instructions on your tickets, Sandile, and you will arrive in London tomorrow to be with your father and your sister. You are a smart boy, Sandile, and I know you will be fine."

She hurriedly explained to Sandile how to read the tickets for his trip, and they rushed off to the boarding gate. When they got to the boarding gate, Sandile held on to his grandmother's hand and would not let go.

"Nkwenkwe, please don't make a scene here or you will attract the wrong kind of attention."

"But Rhundu, I want to take Anelisa with me to America. Please send for her when I am gone."

"Nkwenkwe, you know that will not be possible and I have already asked Mr. Dabula to explain to you why not. You can come back for her when you are a man. Please, my child, we must say our goodbyes now. We don't have much time."

Sandile knew he had to be strong for his grandmother one last time. He could not bear leaving her alone since he had grown up with her since his parents worked so far away from Cofimvaba.

"Rhundu, are you going to be okay without me? Who will fetch the cows from pasture for you, and who will round up your chickens at night into the hen house?"

"Nkwenkwe, do not worry about me. God and the ancestors will take care of me, but now you must go to meet your sister and father. When I see you next time you will be a man and I cannot wait for that time to come. Please, my child, go now, for we are out of time."

Sandile gave his grandmother one last hug and slowly walked with apprehension to the boarding gate. He was leaving the Transkei as a boy, but he vowed to himself that he would one day come back to his village of Cofimvaba as a man. He could not get Anelisa's image out of his mind and felt as if he were betraying her by leaving her behind, but he knew it was no longer safe for him in the Transkei. He cursed the fact that he was a boy and had limited options in how he could respond to his current situation. But he made a deal with himself on that day that he would return to Cofimvaba for Anelisa and Rhundu when he was a man.

Sandile's check in at East London Airport was uneventful. As he approached the x-ray machine to check in his bags, he was asked for his boarding pass to Johannesburg by a tall, stalky man whom he could not identify as white or black, but something in between. He looked at him for a while and then came to the realisation that he was coloured, a term that was used to describe people who were a mixture between black and white in South Africa. The man asked him to step through a rectangular structure, which he said would pick up any steel items that Sandile could have on his person.

As he stepped through, the man followed him to the other side and stopped him. "Young man, it says here that your final destination is London. Can you tell me what the purpose of your trip there is?"

Sandile knew his cover story well, as he had practised it for the last three hours whilst driving to the airport. Mr. Dabula had told him to be as specific about the destination as he could be and, even if the place he was going to did not exist, the border control would have no way of knowing he was not telling the truth.

"Yes, sir, I am on my way to boarding school in the quant region of Plymouth in the United Kingdom. It is about three hours by train from London. When I arrive in London, I will take the train to my boarding school there."

"And who will pick you up at the airport when you arrive in London?"

Sandile did not hesitate, as he knew any hesitation would lead to further questions and, as his grandmother had said, this might lead to unwanted attention. Rhundu was sitting on a bench not far from the check in counter, observing the whole situation. She said the Lord's Prayer over and over again, praying that Sandile would not be referred for further questioning.

"I will be travelling with my headmaster, Mr. Billard. Please, here is his phone number. You may call him if you would like."

Sandile handed the man a UK phone number, which had the number of the hotel his father was in in the UK. His father would confirm that he would be travelling with Mr. Billard to Plymouth boarding school should the security police need to do further checks. The man quickly scanned the phone number and gave it back to Sandile.

"I am sure a boy such as yourself does not have an aptitude for subterfuge. I take it you know how to get to your boarding gate?"

"Yes, sir, it says boarding gate number 2. I will find it just fine."

Sandile turned around to see if his grandmother was still observing him from the bench, but he could not catch sight of her. He panicked a bit, thinking the security police had picked her up and his heart began to race, until he saw her walking out of the front entrance. She looked back at him one more time and he could see that she was crying whilst walking away with a heavy heart.

He had to be strong now as the security police in Johannesburg might be a bit more thorough. He felt a tap on his back as he proceeded to his gate and it was the coloured security policeman. He had something in his hand, which Sandile could not identify, and he thought his cover story was blown and he was going to be arrested.

"Young man, please give me your passport."

Sandile avoided going into a state of panic by thinking about Anelisa and his loving grandmother. He imagined their soothing voices and he was calmed by them.

"Yes, sir. Is there a problem? I told you where my final destination is."

"Nkwenkwe, unless you would like to go through another security check in Johannesburg, I suggest you give me your passport."

Sandile put his bag down on the floor and opened the rear zipper and pulled out his passport from a small compartment in his carry-on bag. The man took the passport and opened it to its last page and stamped it with the object in his hand.

"There. You are now cleared to fly to London without any further security checks."

Sandile held his breath until the man walked away, not knowing how else to hide his fear. When the man was at a safe distance, he took a deep breath and continued walking to Gate 2, which would take him to Johannesburg. He now had to make sure that between East London and Johannesburg he did not do anything that would cause any suspicion.

His grandmother had told him that he should not sit next to any black people at the boarding gate, and he should either sit by himself or next to a white person, which would signal to the security police roving the airport that he was traveling alone. He took a seat next to an old grey-haired white woman who seemed to be lonely. He avoided eye contact with her, so as not be drawn into any conversation where he would have to explain himself. He tried to be as calm as possible, but she could see that he had an air of angst about him and she decided to have a conversation with him.

"Nkwenkwe, so tell me, what is a young man doing travelling on his own?"

Sandile retorted back with a bit of annoyance, "Hello, Mam, how are you?"

"Oh, excuse me, young man, I should have greeted first. My name is Zelda. How are you?"

"Sandile!"

He reached out his hand and shook hers and hoped that would be the end of the conversation. He did not have the patience to explain himself again to someone else after the security police.

"Your English is very good."

How could she tell his English was good, as he had only spoken one sentence to her? She must be after something, he thought. Here he was using her for cover, and she wanted to have a long, drawn out conversation about nothing. He thought about moving away to another seat but knew that would raise suspicion and he did not want to anger her either.

"It's the Queen's English, Mam."

He did not want to give too much away in case he made a mistake with his cover story. But he wanted to be as respectful as possible to not rouse any suspicion. It seemed the old lady got the hint and did not ask Sandile any further questions, or that she had got all the answers she needed from his reply. They sat there in silence until the coloured security officer came over to the old woman and whispered something in her ear. She turned to him and nodded her head and the security officer walked away.

"He was just confirming with me that you are going where you are going. I live in East London, but I spend my workdays in this airport seeing if people are who they say they are and are going where they are meant to be going. People don't really pay too much attention to an old woman sitting by herself at an airport and usually will tell me what I need to hear for my job."

Sandile had to keep up the façade as best as he could. He thought about the British shows that he watched and thought how one of those characters in the show would respond.

"Sounds charming, mam. Noted!"

"You're a bit rude, boy, but I like it. So, the name is Sandile, you say?"

"Yes, mam, it's Sandile."

She gave him a warm, motherly smile, patted him on the shoulder, got up and walked away. Sandile thought about what Mr. Dabula said, that they lived in difficult times. It was starting to dawn upon him just how strange things were in South Africa for black people.

His grandmother had shielded him, along with his village of Cofimvaba, from what apartheid was really like for black people. Now within the last four hours he had experienced the apartheid regime first-hand and it left a sour taste. He wanted to get out of South Africa as soon as possible and be with his family. He was no longer in his village and he felt unsafe.

The loudspeaker announced his flight. He quickly picked up his bag and walked to the check-in counter so that he could be first in line. It was a childish exuberance to get on to the plane, but he did not mind. After all, he was child and should take pleasure in the things children took pleasure in. He was growing up too quickly and he felt the onset of an old soul upon himself with his experiences both in the village and in the last four hours. A middle-aged black man made it to the check-in counter before he did and gave him a penetrating look for him to slow down.

"Slow down, nkwenkwe, there is no rush. The plane will leave only once everyone is on the plane and will not leave anyone behind who has gone through the security checks."

The man rubbed Sandile's head and Sandile felt a calm washing over him. He felt he could trust this man. When the man took his hands off Sandile's head he slowly slid them down to his jacket pocket and put a note in his left pocket.

"Don't look at it now, but when you get to London that is the address where you will find your father, Aggrey."

Sandile's head was spinning. He could not understand how both the security police and the liberation organisations in South Africa had become so efficient and how they could recognise one another. He had never met the man in front of him before and did not know how the man recognised him.

"I was a teacher with your father in the early seventies at the University of the Transkei and you look just like him. I will be your travel companion to Johannesburg to make sure you leave the country safely."

Sandile waited until he got on the plane to open the envelope that the man had given him. In the envelope there was a currency that Sandile had not seen before with the image of a woman wearing a crown on it. It was two hundred British pounds in twenty pound notes and a note with the address of an hotel.

The man who had given him the envelope sat two seats away from him for the trip from East London to Johannesburg, with his eyes set upon him at all times.

Sandile felt the safety of his village during the flight. When Sandile disembarked the plane, the man followed him to his next check-in point from Johannesburg to London. On the way, Sandile stopped by a small food store to buy a chicken pie. He had not eaten since the morning when he'd left his school with Mr. Andreas. The man who was following kept a safe distance while he bought his chicken pie.

"Nkwenkwe, what would you like?"

"One chicken pie please, and one Appletizer."

The woman behind the counter looked at him for a moment and then looked around to see if they were being watched. "Nkwenkwe, you will be on your own for the rest of your trip to London so you must be a man and take care of yourself. The security police looking for your father are everywhere, including London airport. When you get to London airport, tell the arrivals check-in points there that you will be going to meet your father at the hotel in your note. There will be signs at the airport on how to get a taxi. Give the address on the note to the taxi driver. You have more than enough money to pay for a taxi on your arrival."

The woman reached into a small warmer above the cash register and pulled out a warm chicken pie and gave it to Sandile. She then told Sandile to wait whilst she got the Appletizer from the fridge in the back. While Sandile waited, the man who was following came up behind him.

"Don't turn around. Just tell your father when you meet him that his friend Zola sends his greetings. Don't worry about paying for your food and drink, as my wife will not charge you for it since she knows who you are."

Sandile was experiencing his mother's and father's work for the first time and he had a new-found respect for what they did for a living and a greater appreciation of their sacrifice. He now understood why they seldom came home.

"Nkwenkwe, here is your Appletizer and pie. Have a safe trip."

"Thank you, mam, and may God's blessings be upon you."

When Sandile turned around, Zola was nowhere to be found. He walked to the check-in counter and presented his passport and boarding ticket. The security officer flipped the pages to the last one and saw the security stamp. He received another stamp on his passport and the security officer gave him back his passport without saying a word. He simply signalled him to walk through the same rectangular security structure he had walked through in East London and took his bag through the x-ray machine.

"All clear, boy. Proceed to the boarding gate on your ticket!"

Sandile would not make the mistake of sitting next to another white person again, as they could be security police. He slowly walked through the departures lounge looking for his gate, number 27. When he saw it, he continued past it, looking for a solitary seat that had no one sitting next to it. He continued walking to the end of the departure lounge and, when he identified as seat for himself, he walked back to it again. He looked around before taking a seat to see if anyone was looking at him and he saw no signs of danger and took a seat. His flight was departing at 10PM and he had a two-hour wait in the lounge.

He thought about how difficult life had been for his parents and his grandmother. At the same time, he thought about all the white people like Mr. Andreas who were accomplices in the liberation movement in South Africa and how complicated things were in South Africa. At that moment he yearned for freedom from South Africa. He yearned for that feeling of homeliness and safety that he felt in his village and hoped that he would find it in America.

No one came to speak to him while he waited for his flight and he did not see any suspicious eyes glaring at him which could be security police. He decided to take a nap while he waited.

An hour later he was awoken by the loudspeakers announcing his flight. "BA Flight xj6069 to London now boarding."

As Zola had told him to, he took his time walking to the check-in counter so as not to rouse any suspicion. These would be his last steps in his native soil of South Africa for some time to come. He counted each step he made and with each step he thought about Anelisa and Rhundu and their love for him. When he came back, he knew that he would come back not as a boy, but as a man.

Sandile boarded the flight to London without complication. When he got on the plane, he packed his carry-on bag in the compartment above his seat. He was so exhausted from the events of the day that, when he had taken his seat and put on his seatbelt, he passed out for the duration of the ten hour flight. The plane stewardess woke him up for breakfast the next morning. He felt a light tap on his shoulder.

"Excuse me, young man, I did not want to wake you last night, but we will be landing in three hours and we are now serving breakfast. Would you like anything to eat?"

Sandile was captivated by the stewardess' accent and it took him a minute to gather his thoughts and respond to her.

"Yes, mam, I would like something to eat, please."

"Mam? How charming?"

She pulled out a tray with food from her cart and put it on Sandile's food tray. Sandile could not tell if she was taking a liking to him or if she was just doing her job.

"Are you alright, young man? You look a bit stressed."

There was an awkward silence as Sandile thought what he should or should not say in front of the white, middle-aged female passenger next to him.

"I miss my grandmother in the Transkei and also my friend Anelisa, that's all."

"Oh, that's so sweet. I am sure you will see them again soon. Now, please have something to eat because you missed your dinner last night. I did not want to wake you because you looked so peaceful."

"Thank you, mam, it is much appreciated."

"You are so sweet, I just want to gobble you up."

She squeezed Sandile's cheeks and kissed him on the forehead and moved on to the passengers behind him. The middle-aged woman sitting next to him smirked in his direction.

"So, you are quite the charmer. But just know that at home, cross-cultural or interracial relationships are against the law."

Sandile was not quite sure what law he had broken by receiving a kiss on the forehead, but he decided not to pursue the matter any further. After all, she could be a security agent from South Africa. He stayed silent and did not respond to the woman next to him, aside from letting out an uncomfortable smile. It was a power game she was playing and he did not feel like being a part of it.

"What's wrong boy? Don't want to talk to me?"

"No, it's not that.. It's just… My… English… is not that good, and I would rather stay silent, that's all. Unless you would like to speak isiXhosa?"

The woman next to him got the hint that she had offended him with her comments and did not try to make contact with him for the duration of their flight. When the flight landed, the woman sitting next to him tried to show Sandile that she was sorry for offending him and unloaded his carry-on bag from the overhead compartment.

"There you go, young man. No hard feelings. I am sure you understand that I was just pointing out to you how things are at home."

"No offence taken, mam."

Sandile grabbed his bag from her and walked to the entrance of the plane without saying goodbye to the woman. Good riddance, he thought. He could not stand oppression of any kind, whether it came with a smiling face or not. He could tell the laws of the new country were different, because the woman next to him had been insistent in reminding him of how things were at home. She must have been insecure about how things were in England. He came across the air stewardess who had served him his breakfast at the airplane entrance.

"Do you know where you are going, young man?"

Without hesitation he answered her, "Yes, mam, my principal Mr. Billard is waiting for me at the arrivals area. He will travel with me to school in Plymouth."

"Okay. Then I suppose that this is goodbye."

She reached out to hug him and Sandile responded by wrapping his arms around her waist and holding on for a while. Her kindness reminded him of Rhundu and Anelisa.

"Thank you for breakfast, mam, and God's blessings be upon you."

"And you too, young man. Safe travels."

Sandile made his way to the checkout counter, where he had to present his passport yet again. The line moved quickly, and he arrived at the checkout counter to enter the UK. He presented his passport and the man at the checkout counter asked him where he would be staying in the UK. He took out the piece of paper that Zola had given him and gave it to the man at the counter. The man behind the counter glanced at it for a moment and then asked him how long he would be staying. Sandile told him he was on his way to America as per the visa stamp on his passport and he would leave the following morning with his father, whom he was to meet at the hotel indicated on the piece of paper.

He did not mind telling the border officer the truth about his trip, since he no longer felt in danger in this new place. The border officer stamped his passport and pointed him in the direction of the arrivals area. As he walked through the airport, he took in the sights and also noticed the demographic of people was not the same as home. There were a lot more white people than he'd imagined there would be, and he seldom saw a black person.

He followed the signs until he got to the arrivals area and then he started looking around for the signs for the taxi area where he would catch a cab to his father and sister's hotel. He looked around for the signs for taxis but only noticed that there were signs leading to the train station at the airport and became somewhat confused. Had he been misled by Zola and his wife? He thought certainly the security police would find him halfway around the world and use him to get to his father.

He became panic-stricken and could not move. A white man with blonde hair and blue eyes approached him and stuck out his hand to greet Sandile. Sandile became fearful and took a step back in preparation for aggression from the man. The man, sensing Sandile's apprehension reached in his pocket and pulled out a picture. It was Sandile's family picture that had been taken a couple of months ago by his parents.

"Hello, my name is Per. You must be Sandile. Our contact in Cofimvaba Village School, Mr. Dabula, said you would be arriving now. My taxi is waiting outside to take you to your hotel. I suppose Zola gave you some taxi money when you departed from East London to pay for your fare? I know your father from the Swedish Embassy and he will meet you at your hotel later on, after his meetings at the embassy. Your sister will be there too."

Per took out his wallet and showed Sandile his ID. The ID was that of the Swedish Police. Sandile had moved from being panic-stricken to confused.

"I am sure that things must be a bit confusing for you, but a number of your father's associates in the trade unions movement in South Africa have been arrested with the assistance of American intelligence and you will no longer be going to America. Plans have changed and you are going to Stockholm in Sweden tomorrow, with your father and sister. You will meet your mother there. If you follow me to the pay phone, we can call your father and he will confirm this for you."

Sandile had no reason he could come up with not to follow Per to the pay phone. He walked slowly behind him, giving himself a bit of room in case he had to run away. Per picked up the phone and dialled a number and gave the phone to Sandile.

"Hello, Sandile, it's me, Tata. Please go with Per to the hotel. I will meet you there when I am finished my meetings at the Swedish Embassy."

That was all the confirmation that Sandile needed, and he politely smiled at Per and took his hand for him to lead the way. As they walked to the taxi, Per told Sandile about how Swedish trade unions had been supporting his father's work through the trade unions in South Africa for some years now. Per worked closely with the Swedish embassy in London. Six months ago, they were made aware that his mother Phumla was going to travel to the US, but her travels had been compromised. The embassy intercepted her in London and rerouted her to Stockholm, where she had been living and studying finance and strategy for the last five months at Stockholm University.

He told Sandile how the American government had put his mother Phumla and father Aggrey on the terrorist watch list and that, should they have arrived in the US, they would have been deported back to South Africa and charged with crimes against the state, because they were identified as communists.

Sandile tried to pay as much attention to Per as he could, but he would miss a word here and there since Per's accent sounded like fish singing underwater. He, however, understood the gist of Per's explanation and it was enough for him to trust him by getting into the taxi with the man to bring him to his father's hotel. He gave Per the two hundred pounds that he had received from Zola and Per took it and gave him back one hundred and eighty pounds.

"This is the first lesson for you, Sandile. Never do anything or take anything for free. Everything has a cost to it. Remember that, young man, and you will be safe."

Sandile was growing rather apprehensive of Per. If it was his job to pick him up for the embassy, why was it necessary that he should take twenty pounds from him? He understood the idea of paying his own portion, but it was Per's job to take him to his father anyway.

"How far is it to my father's hotel?"

"Not far now. Another twenty minutes and we will be there."

Per noticed Sandile's tone of concern, and he wanted to address it in a constructive manner whilst teaching him about a little bit about Swedish culture.

"Sandile, I know you are young, but you should always seek to take care of yourself. You are a young man and will be a man in a couple of years. After all, in Swedish culture we are all equal and your age does not matter according to the law of Jante."

"Law of Jante? I don't understand. What does that have to do with the twenty pounds you took from me for the fare?"

Per started laughing out loud.

"Sandile, you are in my cab right?"

"Yes, sir."

"Well, a cab needs petrol and you are paying for your share of the petrol."

"Okay, but what is the law of Jante, I don't understand."

Per took a deep breath and tried to come up with the correct words to describe the law of Jante to Sandile.

"Well, Sandile the law of Jante, better known by the term janteloven, can be traced back to Aksel Sandemose, a Danish-turned-Norwegian author, whose works of fiction included references to these 'laws' in the context of small-town Denmark. Janteloven – the law of Jante – at its simplest describes the way that all Scandinavians should behave: putting society ahead of the individual, not boasting about individual accomplishments or being jealous of others and treating one another as equals, and lastly paying one's fair share in society. In short, we are in this cab together and you should pay your fair share of the transport!"

Sandile's confusion was getting the better of him as he tried to remember his geography lessons from school.

"But, sir, I thought we were going to Sweden tomorrow and not Norway or Denmark where the laws of janteloven are from."

"I know it can be a bit confusing, but the Scandinavian nations – Denmark, Norway and Sweden – are pretty similar in terms of culture and over the years the law has been used interchangeably in all the countries alike."

"I think I understand, sir. We are both equal, kind of like egalitarianism."

Sandile's mother had used the word egalitarian in a sentence once when she was speaking to his father with regards to how she expected to be treated in their relationship. He had always wanted to use it in a sentence.

"Clever young man you are, Sandile! Yes, you are sort of right but there are also some nuances about janteloven that you should understand which will assist you in understanding the young children in your age group when you make friends in your new school in Sweden. There are ten general rules to the law of Jante. The ten rules of Jante are: you're not to think *you* are anything special; you're not to think *you* are as good as *we* are; you're not to think *you* are smarter than *we* are; you're not to convince yourself that *you* are better than *we* are; you're not to think *you* know more than *we* do; you're not to think *you* are more important than *we* are; you're not to think *you* are good at anything; you're not to laugh at *us*; you're not to think anyone cares about *you*; you're not to think *you* can teach *us* anything. Although these rules are not literal, they are applied as general rules intended to regulate behaviour or thought in how people relate to one another in Sweden."

These social rules sounded somewhat strange to Sandile, but he made an attempt to memorise them as they were being recited by Per.

"So, in short, sir, I must not stand out and must try to be the same as other children, and be humble."

Per was amazed at how quickly Sandile understood new concepts and did not regret that he had followed his intuition and had addressed him as an equal.

"Sandile, I think if the times we lived in were different and you were a bit older we would have been great friends. But I understand where you get your intellect, as your father has been a challenge for me to get to know as well, since he is so intellectually robust."

Sandile thought perhaps he should say thank you to Per for the compliment, but on the other hand he might be breaking one of the laws of Jante and so he decided to stay humble and not make the conversation about himself but at the same time show Per that he understood the laws.

"Yes, sir, I concur. Often, however, people misinterpret my father's hard work for sharp intellect. I doubt however it is the latter as all human beings are blessed with the same intellect and it's just a matter of how we apply it in our lives."

They had arrived at the Park Plaza Sherlock Holmes Hotel on Baker Street.

"Well, here we are young man. It was nice to have met you. Your father has told the hotel reception that you will be arriving, and they will show you to your room."

"Thanks for the education on the law of Jante, sir. I will keep it in mind when I am in your country!"

Per got out of the driver's seat, walked around the front of the car to the passenger door and opened the door for Sandile. Sandile was a bit confused, since he'd thought they were both equal and he should have opened the door himself. He had a perplexed look on his face, which made Per smile because he knew that Sandile was beginning to deal with paradoxes of Jante Law.

"There is nothing wrong with having manners, young man, even with Jante law in mind. Sometimes, Sandile, and I am not saying you are doing it, people use their intellect to not appreciate other people's gestures of respect and it's important you guard against that."

"Yes, sir, I understand, and thank you for the ride to my hotel. God's blessings be upon you."

"And you too, young man."

Sandile slowly made his way into the hotel whilst watching Per drive away in his taxi. He took a moment to take in the sights of the tall buildings and paved roads everywhere. It was a stark difference from his village of Cofimvaba, which had one paved road with adjoining dirt roads all around. The roads here were very busy with brands of cars that he had never seen before.

The people on the streets walked with a sense of purpose, as if they were in a rush somewhere. It was as if everyone was being marshalled from pillar to post by some invincible force. This was also in contrast to his village where people seemed to loiter about the public areas in town. He thought about the men who would play dice and gamble in front of his grandmother's store the whole day, without a care in the world.

The buildings were also rather high, with numerous levels, and he could remember from a TV show that he had once seen that they were called skyscrapers. He thought a day in London, speaking to the local people, would certainly give him a chance to improve his English and perhaps even a chance to pick up the local accent.

The hotel receptionist had been informed by Sandile's father to give him his own set of keys. His father had also left instructions for Sandile to wait in their hotel room until he and Nobuhlali, Sandile's sister, returned from the Swedish Embassy. Sandile made his way to his room and did not take the time to notice the hotel in great detail. All he could think about was the day he would become a man and return to his village of Cofimvaba for Anelisa.

It was about eight in the morning and his father had informed the receptionist that he would return at about midday, in time for Sandile, Nobuhlali and himself to have lunch. One of Sandile's favourite pastimes was going through his father's work documents when his father was not around. This gave him a better idea of what his father did for a living. Reading his father's work documents was also an opportunity for him to better his English.

The room he was in had one king size bed and two makeshift mattresses on the side of it, which he figured were for him and his sister. He put his bags on the king-sized bed and walked over to the closet to look for his father's bags.

He had some time to kill before lunch and reading through his father's documents would be a chance for him to not think about Anelisa and Rhundu. For a while he could take his mind off thinking about his village of Cofimvaba and perhaps learn enough about what his father was doing to make sense of their move to Sweden.

He found a small leather bag that his father often carried with him on his trips to Johannesburg and began rummaging through it for anything that would assist him to understand what his father was doing at the Swedish Embassy. He unzipped the main zipper of the bag and found a folder marked *Swedish Embassy,* with a six-page document in the folder. The cover page of the document read *Reimagining Africa in the next hundred years.*

He took a seat on the main bed and began slowly reading the document, stopping every now and then to make sense of some words he did not understand. The first reading took him about an hour. He still did not fully understand it and had some questions he reserved for his father for later. After half an hour's rest, he decided to try reading the document again, to see if he could make sense of the parts he did not understand. He decided that he would read the document out loud to himself, so that he could hear the words and hoped that pronouncing them would give them meaning.

He first read the heading out loud: *Reimagining Africa in the next hundred years.* He thought for a minute about what that meant and wondered if his father was part of some Swedish time-travelling project and that perhaps that was the reason he'd had to leave home in such a hurry. This was followed by the body of the document, which he also read out loud.

A Global Bird's Eye View – What will the world look like in 100 years?

The world in 2100 is a vastly different place to today, with advances in medicine and technology completely eliminating the divide between the haves and the have nots. Nanotechnology is adapted to the human genome by African Governments, leading to an increase in human life span of over 300 hundred years. AIDS *is eliminated as a leading cause of death in Africa, leading to one of the youngest and most economically active continents. A corporation between the African and European Union governments, leads to mankind no longer having to do manual labour and finally perfects artificial intelligence. A.I. penetrates every aspect of society, leaving mankind more spare time to pursue the arts and humanities. Africa has managed to consolidate the African Union with one government for Africa with a common monetary Union. The African Rand trades at 1:1 with the Euro as the strongest global currencies.*

Africa in the years 1985 to 2030 starts looking seriously at the issues around continental integration and making integration ideas a reality for Africa beyond common purpose. In the year 2030, there is a continental reorientation of African states, with a move to consolidate Africa under one nation. The African Union manages to do this, but not with a common currency. There is discussion amongst the African states about bringing Africa under a common monetary union but there are dissenting views about which currency to use as the common continental currency. Some of the African states also do not want to abdicate their legislative bodies to the African Union.

There is a new study, which is carried out by the African Union into what is known as Ubuntunomics. Ubuntunomics begins to question the ideas of capitalism and the free market vis-à-vis *the unfair global trading regimes that exist and which impede African growth.*

The African Union, through the study of Ubuntunomics, tries to identify a new financial system that could be used in Africa, which would offset some of the negative consequences of globalisation, capitalism and the free market of the divide between the haves and the have nots.

An interdisciplinary think tank is set up by the African Union comprising top academics, businessmen and women, leading social scientists and artists to look at the ideas around Ubuntunomics and how they can lead to a common monetary union in Africa.

There is consensus, after years of deliberation, that the Rand will be used at the common continental currency. The common monetary union in Africa leads to a resource policy for African nations on how resources are to be exploited for local and global use in African states. By 2035, the African Union is consolidated into a United Africa, with one government for the 54 African nations.

In the year 2030, there is a third global war, over fossil fuels and called the Great War, between some Arab

Nations lead by Iran with the United States. This leads to economic isolation by the United Nations and participant nations. China tries to mediate during the Great War but is pulled into an armed conflict by American sectarian right-wing terrorists who bomb the Chinese parliament, believing China is not neutral. This was as a result of China developing and switching to renewable energy sources and away from fossil fuels in 2028. China refuses to share its technology with the US but rather uses it to develop African nations and fast track their development, with the trade-off being African resources.

There is a massive resource shortage in China in the years 2025 to 2035, leading to China developing a more intimate development relationship with Africa to meet its resource needs. The United States is forced after the Great War to step down from the United Nation Security Council, and the rest of the United Nations participating nations place economic sanctions on it. China, after the Great War, becomes the largest donor to the United Nations and lobbies to move the headquarters of the UN to Beijing.

Arab nations and America, not having made the switch to renewable energy sources, sign a new compact with one another to form their own version of the UN called the Pax Americana, headquartered in Dubai, and withdraw from the UN. Due to the corporatisation of Middle East and American politics, they find it difficult to move over to renewable energy sources because of the economic hold of some of the biggest oil producers not wanting to make the switch away from fossil fuels.

In 2035, American and Arab nations as a result suffer hyperinflation, leading to a consideration of a bailout by China. China opts to keep targeted sanctions on America and selected Arab Nations.

By 2040, Africa has the highest economic growth patterns in the world, with 25% GDP growth per annum as a result of coming up with a continental policy for its resources, which are largely being consumed by China, whose economic growth patterns have stalled as a result of a further 500 million people being brought out of poverty and the servicing of a larger population by government and need for natural resources. Food prices escalate out of control in China and there is not enough space to house its growing population. Africa becomes the saviour for China by offering food at affordable prices and also providing some arable land for Chinese multinationals to grow crops.

America and some Arab nations also lobby Africa aggressively in the hopes of being able to have access to some of its raw materials and arable land for food growth. By 2040, over 60% of the world's food emanates from Africa, along with 50% of the global freshwater needs. The resource scarcity in the world propels Africa to having the strongest international currency in the world with some global trading being done in Rand terms. The Africa rising story becomes a global reality.

In 2050, an atomic research institute in Switzerland discovers how to open up wormholes as means of interstellar travel. Humanity identifies a number of new planets that host life and are inhabited by human-like beings. There is a resource shortage in some of those planets and a deal is made by African states for them to settle on the African continent because Africa still has vast tracts of uninhabited land whilst the rest of the world is suffering from over population. The extra-terrestrials bring new technology to Africa, leapfrogging Africa 100 years ahead of the other global nations.

Africa in 2055 signs a development treaty with the European Union for free labour movement between the EU and Africa. By 2065, Africa and the EU are the most developed areas in the world. A new Global Development Bank is started in Johannesburg to facilitate economic and technological development to Europe and the rest of the world.

By 2070, the United Nations collapses due to underfunding by the Chinese government and a lack of global buy in. A new global governance organisation emerges called Nubian Parliament, which is based in Cape Town, South Africa, with Africa, Latin America, the EU and Japan being the only four members of its security council.

Africa and the EU send peacekeeping troops to America, Middle East and China to avert another global conflict as a result of the scarcity of global resources. The year 2100 is the year of convergence, where nanotechnology is combined with the human genome, thereby exponentially increasing the human life span by 300 years.

Capitalism, as a result of A.I., is restructured and a new form of economic management appears out of Africa called Ubuntu Capitalism. The monetary system is done away with and a more egalitarian system of economic management is introduced where people get equal credits, no matter what their employment is.

Innovation is run and controlled by nation states with massive benefits for the global population, from free housing, made and designed by A.I., to free universal education across the board. Food is no longer a paid for commodity and is free. Because of the longer life span of people, procreation is tightly state controlled, with each family being able to have two children every 150 years.

By 2100, the world has realised its vision of peaceful co-existence with the last global war being the Great War of 2030. Humanity and extra-terrestrial life live side by side in harmony. The African version of Ubuntu Capitalism goes global and global markets are shut down and remembered only as vestiges of the past. The world remembers the century as an African century and academic institutions all around the world are set up to study African philosophy and how to entrench it in their societies as a way of creating equitable and sustainable societies. Africa is the world's moral superpower in the new century.

Africa in a Nutshell – Africa emerges into a global superpower

After the Great War in 2030, African governments consolidate the African continent in 2035 by creating one country with a common currency with all the African countries being member states. A governance body is set up by the Nubian Parliament to carry out African continental elections with the sitting president of Africa sitting at the Nubian Parliament headquarters in Cape Town South Africa. A common resource policy for all African nations is developed for the beneficiation and selling of African raw materials. Most raw materials are now processed and beneficiated in Africa rather than taken abroad as raw materials and then sent back to Africa as finished goods.

There are new oil and gas finds from Egypt to Cape Town. However, Africa is only able to sell the oil and gas to North America and Middle East since China, Africa and the EU have moved on to renewable energy sources.

Food security and water scarcity become major issues in the world, particularly in China and America, and Africa is called on to provide China and the US with food aid and clean water.

By 2040, as a result of continental co-operation, Africa has a growth rate of 25% per annum with 70% of global raw materials along with 60% of global arable land and 50% of global fresh water. New learning institutions are set up in Africa around Ubuntunomics to look at indigenous African methodologies of governance and market participation. By 2045, Africa has 20 universities rated in the top 20 places to study in the world for a new global perspective. Students from all around the world, particularly Asia and Europe, are flocking to Africa to receive their tertiary education. Africa becomes a melting pot of cultures and has cities that are the most culturally dynamic in the world.

In 2050, Africa is the natural place to settle because of its dynamic education systems, multicultural societies and also available land. The integration between humanity and the new alien arrivals is quick and Africans open up their societies, cultures and homes to the new arrivals.

Africa cannot grow without the rest of the world and thus makes a technology trade agreement with the EU in 2055 that leads to Africa and Europe being the two most developed continents in the world by 2065. Peacekeeping initiatives are organised throughout the world by Africa and Europe, whilst they decide how they are going to bring the rest of the world up to speed in a sustainable manner with the new technology boom that is taking place in Africa and Europe. This leads to the establishment of a global technology development bank, with the Nubian Parliament in Cape Town, to monitor global development.

The Nubian Parliament in Cape Town recommends that the world governments start using Ubuntu Capitalism and a gradual move is made from the free-market capitalist system to Ubuntu Capitalism. By 2095, the African Technology Bank, with the assistance of the EU, have brought development parity to the world, along with the new economic innovations in Ubuntu Capitalism. Nations around the globe have equal development, and food security and water are no longer an issue as they are made free by the African governments.

The creation of A.I. by an African government research institute has brought about free housing for all to be developed by the A.I., which means people are no longer in debt to financial institutions and having pay off their bonds for more than two decades. Banks are transformed into credit institutions and act on behalf of the state in terms of issuing out and monitoring equal credit to all its citizens.

With the birth of renewable energy sources, cars are also banned and everyone has to use emission-free public transport. By the time of the convergence in 2100, Africa has donated a lot of intellectual capital to the world in order to imbue global governance systems with the spirit of African values and principles. Africa leads the convergence with nanotechnology, wiping out all diseases and birth defects.

Convergence drastically changes man's sense of meaning and why we are here on earth, and global peace is achieved and maintained by the Nubian Parliament.

Human beings have a lot more time to discover their passions and hobbies. After the nanotechnology convergence of 2100, in the search for meaning by humanity African learning institutions are spread out throughout the globe, attracting the best minds to study indigenous African thought. The pyramids and the ancient sites in Northern Sudan are the major source of inspiration for the new topics of studies, which are emerging throughout the world in studying African philosophy. Africa becomes the global moral and religious superpower as a new religion forms throughout the globe based on African Gods, which makes a seamless integration with the other main religions, Christianity, Islam and Judaism.

From 2100 to 2120, African religion becomes the dominant world religion, with some sporadic sects of

Christianity, Judaism and Islam still existing. The cult of money is outlawed on the globe and markets, reserve banks and stock exchanges become museums for students to study about the past economic systems and their failures. Peace is achieved and maintained by highly regulated societies which practise highly centralised and bureaucratised governance models but still offer democracy as a form of governance. The African gift to humanity of Ubuntu becomes immortalised in a global holiday called Ubuntu Humanity Day.

African Political Changes

The establishment of the Nubian Parliament forces African countries to revisit their governance systems and there is a continental review of democracy in African states. With Africa historically having used governance systems that were not African in nature – such as communism, socialism and democracy – a move is made to develop indigenous means of African governance. A mixture of a continental monarchy and social democracy is developed to meet the needs of a new and complex Africa. Various Africa indigenous kings make up the executive advisory and head up the legislature of the Nubian parliament. These kings are sourced from every African country with each African nation being able to vote in three kings per country to the executive advisory. Each nation has a chance to vote in the kings they would like from their nation to be deployed to the Nubian parliament to compose the executive advisory legislature.

These kings support and advise an African president who is voted in democratically through a continental democratic election process. It then becomes the role of the executive advisory to form a legislature, which is comprised of elected headmen and chiefs from the various regions around Africa. The executive advisory selects ten chiefs and headmen as representatives from each country in Africa.

The emergence of an African religion assists the African nations to be able to come up with a new continental constitution that is based on African cultural practices and ways of governance. It is not written like the British Magna Carta but interpreted through the various governance institutions that represent the legislative body of governance, and through precedent. African children are taught to memorise various case studies from their primary education, which represent the foundations of an oral constitution.

The judiciary, in order to guarantee its independence, has a separate process from the executive and legislative process for how judges are decided upon. A judicial adjudication committee is set up in each African country, composed of retired presidents and executive advisory members, who decide on which judges to appoint to which courts in the Nubian Parliament. These judges, who form the judiciary, are ratified in their posts through local referendums in each of their constituencies in which the voting public ratifies them into their posts. African governance interventions are so successful that other nations also decide to have a symbiosis between traditional governance and social democracy. Africa truly becomes a beacon of hope and innovation for the world to follow in terms of its governance structures, and how it elects it various representatives of governance.

Africa becomes a knowledge society

The changes in Africa in the next hundred years allow for it to emerge as a knowledge-based society, with most of its services focused on the development and trading of indigenous knowledge in the governance, financial and medical fields. Africa has moved out of the areas of primary production, to knowledge development and production, and sells its services to other nations. Indigenous knowledge becomes the most valuable African commodity for the survival of African nations.

Indigenous knowledge production also deals with moral challenges that Africa faces in the next hundred years of its responsibility to the global questions around nano integration and globalisation. The discontents of globalisation and its historical disadvantages towards unfair trade regimes for Africa and developing nations are sorted out through various indigenous interventions by the African continent. These interventions are based on the equal sharing of knowledge through the principles of Ubuntu and Ubuntunomics, which is a financial system developed in Africa with indigenous African ideals and principles. African indigenous thought becomes a true reflection of some of man's greater questions of why we are here on earth and answers some of the age-old questions around the meaning of the existence of man.

Egalitarian societies spring up all over the world, based on African indigenous knowledge and its application. The future questions that emerge as a result of indigenous African knowledge and its global use, centre around the challenge of the eradication of the knowledge divide around the world and bring all nations in parity with one another in terms of knowledge production and its application. A new global collective consciousness emerges as a result of the contribution of indigenous African knowledge systems, which further leads to a new global intellectual convergence based on African principles of management.

The gains made by mankind as a result of African intellectual capital lead to a new age of intellectual renaissance, where new theorems are produced with regards to mankind's proximity to the universe. African indigenous knowledge systems usher in an African age which brings a new sense of hope and optimism to humanity, which in turn leads to global stability in the first era of global peace, coexistence and knowledge sharing on a global scale. Africa yields a new spiritual dividend for a new era, which is shared with the world as the world looks to an era beyond convergence.

The African generation of the 21st century yields champions of change, who are remembered as the foundations of the birth of a new African era. Africa redefines its place in history, not as the Dark Continent but the centre of new global hope based on indigenous African knowledge.

Africa, a future-focused society

Africa in the next hundred years starts being a future-focused society and starts planning what Africa will look like in the next 1 000 years. Institutions are set up to investigate what alternative futures Africa has within the next thousand years. The question that African starts trying to answer is: what kind of society does Africa have beyond a knowledge sharing society? With the integration of humanity and nanotechnology, human beings have a much longer life span to be able to live learn and contribute to the intellectual questions of the continent. The collective thinking power of the continent is dedicated to the planning of a future Africa and its place in the world.

As humanity advances, the questions of our existence and our proximity to the universe become more complex. When children enter basic education, they are taught scenario-planning processes in order to be able to add novel ideas to the future society that they would like to live in. Secondary and tertiary education teaches students the philosophical responsibilities of the convergence process with nanotechnology. Philosophical themes that emerge in secondary and tertiary education are around how far humanity is willing to integrate with nanotechnology and what it is that defines humanity in the new age of convergence.

Within society as a whole, there are a few dissenting voices to the convergence process, but there are more philosophical questions that arise than dissenting voices. The age of convergence brings about a new collective consciousness amongst humanity, which only increases the questions about human self-determination, its potential and its limitations. The limitations on thinking and capacity to hold acquired information for human beings becomes a non-issue and the learning process is radically transformed and accelerated as a result of the convergence process.

Learning institutions are focused on the future and also on managing the moral questions that arise for humanity as a result of convergence. The biggest moral question that humanity tries to answer is to what extent human beings should integrate with nanotechnology and what the potential of consciousness is. These are the great themes of a future-focused Africa beyond the age of convergence.

The pace of development in Africa speeds up to an exponential pace, where societies are changing, innovating and adapting to the change and innovation by the second. Human collective consciousness grows in leaps and bounds as new philosophical questions emerge and are collectively addressed in the future-focused society. It is an age of human development such as has never been seen or imagined before in history.

African societies move beyond the limitations of intergenerational thinking, to thinking centuries ahead of time, which radically transforms the pace of human development.

When he finished reading the document out loud for the second time, an hour had passed and he still did not have any further insight into what his father was working on with the Swedish Embassy. He had more questions than he had answers, but at least his mind was no longer focused on leaving his village of Cofimvaba, and he was not thinking about Anelisa and Rhundu. He would, however, have to come up with a unique way to ask his father questions about his document, which did not get him into trouble for going through his bags.

He put the file back into his father's bag but not before noticing a book in the bag with the title *South Africa Beyond Apartheid*, written by his father.

He decided to take a nap and await the arrival of his sister and father from the Swedish Embassy so that he could ask his father questions that would give him clarity on exactly what he did.

A half an hour passed by and then he heard the sound of keys battling to open the door, which made him sit up from his bed. He looked at the keyhole and noticed that he had left his own keys in the keyhole and the person trying to open the door would not be able to get in from the other side. Because he had been napping, he did not know what time it was and he still thought it was early in the morning. Sudden paranoia gripped him, and he thought perhaps the security police had found him. He walked up to the door and put his right ear against the door to see if he could hear any voices he recognised.

In a small voice he whimpered, "Yes, who is it?"

"Sandile, it's Tata. Please open the door."

A wave of elation came over him, but he suppressed it, still fearing the worst. After all, perhaps the security police could mimic people's voices. He slowly opened the door and left a small opening through which he peeked to confirm it was his father and sister. He flung the door open and hugged his father. He hung on for a few moments longer than usual and his father surmised that the trip to London had been mentally taxing for his son.

His sister Nobuhlali also hugged him whilst he was hugging his father. She was glad that her family was almost back together again. They were only left with the prospect of a two-hour flight to Sweden, where they would meet up with their mother Phumla.

"Okay, children, let us go inside the room. We don't want to attract the wrong attention."

Sandile had heard that statement before from his grandmother Rhundu at the airport and he knew that they still had to be careful in this new place until they got to their final destination, Sweden. Sandile and Nobuhlali took a seat on the king-sized bed and awaited instruction from their father.

"Children, we will be going to have lunch in the hotel restaurant and then I have to go back to the Swedish Embassy to give a presentation."

Nobuhlali noticed the open closet and knew that Sandile had been going through her father's documents again. She knew well enough that he liked doing it in secret and would not give him away, but she was always alarmed at how sloppy he was. He always left clues to what he was doing and this upset Nobuhlali and she would often tell him that his lack of attention to detail would be his undoing.

"Children, I know this must be a confusing time for you and I know you have a lot of questions. Let's address them now whilst we wait for lunch. When we get downstairs, we will have to be careful what we talk about and act like any ordinary family having lunch in a hotel restaurant in London."

Nobuhlali seemed content with the explanation that her father had given her whilst they'd travelled together. Sandile, on the other hand, had a different travel experience, which only resulted in more questions for his father. He raised his hand to let his father know he had a question.

"Yes, nkwenkwe, what do you want to ask?"

"Tata, you told us before that you work for the trade unions, but your friends said you taught at the University of the Transkei."

Sandile knew that was not the question he wanted to ask his father, but he wanted to take his attention away from the fact that he had read his documents before asking him the questions that were on his mind.

"Yes, nkwenkwe, I did work for the University of the Transkei in the early seventies. However, I found a lot of my students were getting arrested and detained in Johannesburg for political activism, so I moved to Johannesburg to assist with the liberation movement and workers' rights. Do you understand?"

Sandile could not contain himself and blurted out, "Tata, have you travelled into the future at the Swedish Embassy?"

His sister Nobuhlali could not hold her laughter in and started laughing out loud in an uncontrollable way. She was two years older than Sandile but far more mature than he was as a result of the conservative Catholic convent school she attended. Her written and spoken English were also better than Sandile's and she would often assist him to understand the English language through correcting him whenever he misunderstood a phrase or did not know the meaning of specific words.

"Ntobi, please don't laugh at your brother."

Nobuhlali was laughing at Sandile, not because of the immaturity of his question but because he had given away that he had been going through his father's documents. Aggrey knew how inquisitive his son was and decided he would entertain his question and not reprimand him for going through his bag.

"Children, I want to be very transparent with you both as to why your mother and I had to leave the country.

Aggrey's tone became very serious and Sandile and Nobuhlali sat upright at the edge of their seats, as if preparing to salute a military superior. Both Nobuhlali and Sandile responded in unison, "Yes, Tata."

"Your mother and I were the co-authors of a book called *South Africa beyond Apartheid*. Your mother did the research for the book with some of her associates from Peking University in China. She then gave the research to us in the trade unions who were working with some American non-governmental agencies and we put it together in a book and circulated it to various members of liberation organisations.

"We did not know until some months later that the American NGOs had submitted the book to members of the security branch and therefore we had to cancel our trip to the US because we would not be safe there because we were labelled as communists and were put on the terrorist watch list in America.

"When the South African government heard about the book, they labelled it as subversive, thinking that it was intended to overthrow the government. Your mother and I were then labelled as communists and terrorists and that is when we decided that your mother had to leave the country six months ago, because our family was no longer safe from the apartheid regime.

"In her travels to China, your mother befriended some Swedish students who took an interest in our work and then connected us with the Swedish government, and they invited your mother to continue her studies in Sweden and for me to work with the Swedish trade unions on my trade union work."

Aggrey was still not addressing Sandile's question of time travel, and he was becoming mildly impatient.

"But, Tata, what about the time travel? How do you know what is going to happen in the future?"

"Patience, young man, I will get to that."

He looked at Sandile and Nobuhlali for a moment, trying to gauge if they understood him so far. They both said in unison again, "Yes, Tata."

Aggrey collected himself and thought how he was going to answer Sandile's question in a way that made sense to the children and help them to understand his work on the future with Swedish trade unions.

"Children, to put it simply, when the prime minister of Sweden Olof Palme became head of state of Sweden, he started a research program for Africa. The research project was called Africa 2100. He invited trade union members from all over Africa to research and develop themes about how Africa would look in the future beyond the year 2100. We in South Africa were also asked to add our views to how Africa would look like beyond colonialism and apartheid, well into the future.

"The research group has been put together by people from different African nations who refer to themselves as futurists or students of the future. Simply put, we put together scenarios of what alternative African futures could be and then we discuss them with various members of the Swedish government in order that they be prepared for alternative futures for the African continent.

"The scenario you read, Sandile, was not the future but a statement of what an alternative future might look like. We have many of these scenarios within the research group and we discuss all of them at the embassy. For example, this afternoon I must go and present my alternative scenario of the future. It is not that I have travelled there, but I am extrapolating from current sociological, economic and political developments what the future might be like. It is what we refer to as futurology.

"Your mother and I and some of our research partners are going to put all of our work together in a document called NEPAD or New Partnership for African Development. When your mother finishes her studies, and I am done with my work with my African partners in the African research program put together by Prime Minister Olof Palme, we will then circulate the NEPAD document to various African governments for implementation. We anticipate that our work will take us about five years to finish, so we will be Sweden for the next five years, children. I hope you understand."

Five years did not seem that long to Sandile. By the time his parents were finished their work, he would be a man and could go back to his village for Anelisa and his grandmother.

Although Nobuhlali and Sandile did not fully understand their father, especially when it came to NEPAD, they nodded their heads in unison in order to give their father some reprieve and time to rest before lunch. They could see how stressed he was about their trip and his work and they wanted to give him some time to relax. Nobuhlali could not, however, help herself and had to ask one more question before her father took his rest.

"Tata, so this NEPAD document is a plan for black people in Africa?"

Aggrey again sought the best words to explain to his daughter the meaning to her question. "Honey, kind of. It's a plan for a united Africa beyond colonialism and apartheid when white and black people live in peace and not conflict."

Nobuhlali was intellectually succinct and like her brother Sandile had the ability to understand complicated concepts. She continued with her questions.

"So, the Americans are bad and that is why we are not going to live there for you and Mama to do your work?"

"No, honey, they are not necessarily bad people. It's just that they don't know whom they are supporting. On one hand, their NGOs – or non-governmental organisations – give us financial and research support, but their government gives intelligence support to the white apartheid security regime which suppresses black people. And on the African continent their government supports the trade liberalisation and privatisation which are economic prescriptions that make African countries poor, through selling off their national assets like communications and energy companies and also opening up their markets to meet the debt positions which they incur with America and which America has been granting since the end of colonialism.

"Also, another issue is that Africa is not allowed to develop its own industries as a result of American debt, as it has to send its raw materials to the West and it comes back as finished goods for which Africans must pay a premium while servicing high interest loans from America. It is what many researchers call the debt or dependency trap."

Aggrey was aware that he had lost one of his children in the explanation, as Sandile was now looking out the window and he seemed to be somewhere far away.

Nobuhlali continued. "Trade liberalisation and privatisation. I am not sure I understand."

"Honey, your mother will explain it to you in more detail, but it simply means that the Americans want African minerals for cheap and then they want Africa to sell their government businesses to private industry as well, which means they will not be able to generate money from them to take care of their people and develop their countries. At the end then, they want to offer us money called AID to make up for the sale of African government businesses for African governments to be able to survive. It's a dependency trap that will only make Africa poorer."

Nobuhlali sensed her father was tired and needed some rest and she relented with her questions. "Okay, Tata, I think I understand. The Americans want our gold and diamonds for cheap and for us to be dependent on them through AID."

"Yes, honey, in short that is it, but the Americans are not bad people. It's just that, with resource scarcity in the world, nations like America develop mercenary approaches to getting their hands on African resources. Your mother will explain it to you and your brother much better than I can, honey. Let's get some rest now, before lunch."

Sandile suddenly gained interest in the conversation as he was also starting to make sense of the discussion. "But Tata, does China also not want African gold and diamonds for cheap?"

"Nkwenkwe, all you need to know about China is that for now they are willing to pay more for African minerals than America, and also they don't get politically involved in suppressing black African people in the African countries that they assist. They seem to be a willing development partner for Africa, although they also want African resources."

Aggrey suddenly felt very tired and crept into the king-sized bed, in between Sandile and Nobuhlali, and closed his eyes. Nobuhlali rested her head on her father's chest whilst Sandile continued looking out the window, daydreaming about a far-off place. His mind took him back to the village of Cofimvaba, where he could smell the grass in the town park mixed with scents of cow dung. He sat there staring at the window for half an hour, thinking that he would never get the chance to go to the mountains with the other boys in his village.

He thought about whether or not they would consider him a man when he came back to his village if he got circumcised in a Swedish hospital. He was reminded of the words of Mr. Dabula that "the ancestors would forgive him for not going to the mountains because of the times they lived in". He thought about the work his father and mother were doing, both in South Africa and Africa, and was somewhat amazed by the commitment to their cause. They had left the country of their birth and had both committed to fighting injustice with the God-given tools that they had.

He thought about all of the other African families who'd had to leave their countries of birth during apartheid and years before during colonialism. His mother and father had educated him and his sister Nobuhlali about African colonial states and the subjugation of African people across the continent. His father Aggrey would always tell him and his sister how he considered himself to be a pan Africanist in that he believed the fortunes of Africa were dependent on all African nations achieving liberation. South Africa would be the last African nation to achieve its independence.

He had not fully understood his father's explanation of his work, but he knew his mother would explain it to his sister and him when they got to Sweden. She would bring more clarity to his father's explanation, since she was very good at making complex subjects easily understood for him and his sister.

An hour later, his sister and father awoke and it was a little after midday. They descended to the first floor on the elevator from where their room was on the second floor. Both Sandile and his sister's attention was focused on not attracting attention to themselves and assisting their father to make sure that they seemed like any normal family on holiday in Europe in the summer. They spoke English amongst themselves and kept their eyes down as they walked through the hallways of the hotel.

Lunch was uneventful and they did not speak that much, whether about their trips to get to London or the last part of their journey to Sweden. After lunch, Aggrey walked Sandile and Nobuhlali back the room and asked that they stay there until he returned from his presentation at the Swedish Embassy. Nobuhlali fell asleep immediately and slept until the early evening, when her father returned for dinner. Sandile, on the other hand, sat at the same place on the bed he had sat in before lunch, and continued to stare out the window and dream of far-off places in his village of Cofimvaba.

He thought about what he would say to Anelisa when he returned a man. He thought about his grandmother and if she would be okay without him there to herd the cows and put the chickens in the hen houses in the evenings. For the rest of the afternoon, he sat in a trance, imagining the future, his manhood and his return to his village of Cofimvaba.

Their father Aggrey had left the hotel with their passports and told them that he would have to get visas for them to enter Sweden. Sandile thought it quite strange that they needed a piece of paper to enter foreign nations. He was reminded of the American visa that his grandmother had got him and how he would never use it. He started to be fearful for his grandmother and thought, if his family did not end up going to America, perhaps the American security agents would arrest his grandmother for misleading them. He sat up, staring at the window, concerned for his grandmother's safety until his father returned.

When his father returned with their Swedish visas, Sandile waited patiently for his father to close and lock the door in case they were overheard by someone walking past their hotel room.

"Tata, will grandmother not get in trouble with the American security agents."

"Nkwenkwe, why is that?"

"Because she got me a visa for America, and I will not be going there."

His father was impressed by his concern for his grandmother and Sandile's understanding of the situation that they were in and hugged him.

"Nkwenkwe, don't worry. It was Mr. Dabula who got you the visa through an NGO which gives financial support to your school Village. I am sure the NGO will think we were caught by the South African security police and will not make an issue of it. So, don't worry. I think your grandmother will be fine."

Sandile also wanted to confirm what Mr. Dabula had told him about manhood, since Anelisa and his grandmother were foremost on his mind.

"Tata, Mr. Dabula said I don't have to go to the mountain to be a man and that I can go to hospital. I want to go back to Cofimvaba when I am a man for Anelisa."

His father knew how close his son and Anelisa were, and he had watched them grow from infants to young children together.

"Nkwenkwe, you are already brave enough to be a man, but yes, you will have to go to a hospital to be circumcised and the ancestors will forgive you for it."

Sandile had got the answer he had been looking for and his father's comments allayed his concern. He imagined his future of becoming a man in a Swedish hospital and for a moment he was content to be so far away from Cofimvaba.

That evening, Aggrey ordered in for himself and the children. They ate and watched some TV and fell asleep early at seven. They were all exhausted from their travels and the subterfuge and the level of care involved. They had got to England not only as a result of their own efforts, but also through individuals in the liberation movement like Rhundu, Mr. Dabula, Zola and his wife, and Mr. Andreas.

They were willing accomplices in a difficult time to ensure their family was safe on their travels out of South Africa.

That evening, Sandile woke up at midnight because he had a dream that would not allow him to go to sleep. In his dream, he had been circumcised in a Swedish hospital and had returned home to his village of Cofimvaba. However, on his arrival his peers had insisted on calling him inkwenkwe because he had not been to the mountains. When he went to see Anelisa, she was also pregnant with an older man's child and she could not be with him. She had moved on.

He sat up for an hour, thinking to himself what the meaning of his dream was. His grandmother had told him that dreams were the way in which angels communicated with humans and they were narrating God's message. He knew he could not ignore the dream, but his father had confirmed that the ancestors would forgive him for being circumcised in a hospital because of the times. This thought allayed some of his concerns, although he was still worried about Anelisa and her getting pregnant by an older man.

His grandmother had sent his sister away to a Catholic school to avoid her getting pregnant at an early age like the other young girls in his village. He thought if only he could get hold of his grandmother and ask her to send Anelisa now to that same Catholic school, perhaps she could avoid her fate in his dreams.

The following morning he awoke and narrated his dream to his father and sister over breakfast. His father's position was that there was little people could do to avoid their fate. The ancestors, with the assistance of the angels, revealed our fate so that we could be better prepared for it in the future. His final analysis was that life happens, whether we like it or not, and we have to accept it.

Sandile had a very difficult time digesting this notion. Would he be an inkwenkwe to his peers all his adult life for getting circumcised at a hospital, and would Anelisa get pregnant by another man and not wait for him to return to Cofimvaba? The future he imagined was unpalatable to him and his dream would force him in his time away from Cofimvaba to lament about a future with Anelisa.

5

Per came to pick up Sandile, his father and sister early in the morning at six for an eight o'clock flight to Stockholm. On the way to the airport, Sandile had feelings of emotional freedom that he was no longer responsible for Anelisa's future and that another man would come and fill the void he had left in her life by leaving their village. His manhood would not be defined by going back to his village for her. He resigned himself to the idea that, even though he would not be with Anelisa as his wife, she would always hold a special place in his heart as his sister and close friend. He would always have her interests at heart.

However, what he could not resolve in his mind was that in his dream his peers would refer to him as inkwenkwe during his adult life. This idea taunted his thoughts. He thought perhaps there was some way to augment the future he had dreamt about.

His sister was sitting in the front seat with Per and he and his father were sitting together in the back seat. He queried his father again on the taxi ride to Heathrow airport.

"Tata, in my dream, aside from Anelisa being pregnant, when we are older the other boys in my class were also calling me inkwenkwe, even after I had been circumcised in a Swedish hospital."

Per overheard his question to his father and blurted out, "Oh yes, the Xhosa rights of passage. You know, Sandile, most children in Sweden get circumcised soon after they are born, if at all. Manhood in Sweden is not defined by the 'great chop', but how you relate to others as equals. Both women and men are equal, and the rights of passage are rather to be defined by one's proximity to one's family and community."

Sandile's sister Nobuhlali also overheard the conversation. Sandile was not sure he wanted to proceed with it. His father Aggrey saw the look of apprehension on Sandile's face and also did not respond to Per, but Per kept on going with his train of thought.

"In the Konungariket Sverige, things are much more egalitarian and I would be as bold as to say different in terms of the cultural rights of passage to manhood."

Sandile's father decided to change the conversation, as he was also a bit confused by Per statement.

"Per, kindly explain to us what is Konungariket Sverige?"

"Oh, sorry for that. Sometimes I don't pay attention and I mix Swedish with my English without noticing. It means the Kingdom of Sweden, since we have a monarchy. Today, Sweden has a constitutional monarchy, which means that the monarch's duties are regulated by the constitution. According to the Swedish constitution, the king as head of state is the country's foremost representative and symbol. The king's duties are primarily ceremonial and representative, but we still refer to Sweden as the Kingdom of Sweden. A lot of families have a picture of the royal family in their restrooms."

Per let out laughter after his comments, as if Sandile, his father and sister were meant to understand the joke. Somehow, Nobuhlali picked up on the joke and laughed along with Per.

"Truly egalitarian in a weird way, with the pictures of the king and queen in their toilets."

Sandile and his father decided not to pay him any mind and returned to their conversation. Sandile's father also wanted to abate some of Sandile's fears. He also showed him that discussing the matter in front of his sister was not an affront to his manhood. He decided to take a serious and frank tone, since he thought that was how Sandile needed to be addressed, otherwise he would vacillate with this same issue throughout his childhood.

"Sandile, as you know I am from Ghana and as a result of you being my son you are Ghanaian. Although your mother is my wife and I respect Xhosa tradition, I am not bound by it entirely, but I strongly believe you should be circumcised. In our culture, children are circumcised after they are born, not as a matter of tradition but in order to avoid some infections when they are older. I know that this ritual is important to you, and I will abide by your mother's culture. You will be circumcised in a hospital and you should accept that!

"For me, manhood is not defined by your circumcision but, as Per said, by your proximity to family and community. You are also now a global citizen and you should develop beyond some of the cultural limitations that hold back your development. Also, with regards to what your peers said to you in your dream, who are they to judge your path to manhood? I suggest you come to a resolve now that you will not go to the mountain and be settled with that thought in your heart, because it is not your destiny. After all, I am sure the ancestors will forgive you."

Nobuhlali understood that the idea of manhood and circumcision were becoming an unhealthy obsession for Sandile and concurred with her father. "I agree with Tata, Sandile. You are half Xhosa and half Ghanaian, and you should try and let this issue go. There are so many old inkwenkwe's in Cofimvaba because they are scared to go to the hospital, let alone go to the mountains."

Aggrey was rather troubled at his daughter's comment and how she came about that information. He lamented the idea that he had not been able to spend more time with his children and they were growing up without his guidance. He was about to ask Nobuhlali how she knew that some men went uncircumcised, but she anticipated his question.

"Some of the male teachers in my school referred to some of the other teachers as inkwenkwes and that's how I know. More than half of my male teachers were not circumcised."

Aggrey refrained from his question and rather continued the thread that Per had started. "So, Per, this Kingdom of

Sweden of yours, what should we expect as foreigners in your land?"

"Ah, yes, I am glad you asked, Aggrey. Expect to be welcomed, for your cultures to be accepted and respected and for you to feel at home. After all, we are a small population in Sweden, and everyone knows everyone. Also expect to be an equal within the law of Jante."

Sandile was looking off into the distance though the car window.

"Rhundu always has always told me that I am a responsible young man, so perhaps going to the mountains should not be foremost on my mind, nor the actual circumcision, whether in a hospital or on a mountain, should not be what I should focus on."

His father thought perhaps he was not able to reach him to make him understand that going to the mountains would not happen for him. He wanted him to know that there was nothing wrong with going to the hospital to be circumcised.

Aggrey and Nobuhlali understood that the idea of circumcision and manhood was something that had been drummed into his mind by the other men in Cofimvaba and he was not going to let it go so easily.

"Well, ladies and gentlemen, we are at the airport now and you must begin the last part of your journey to the Kingdom of Sweden. It was nice to have met you all and I think you are a wonderful family and will fit in well in the Kingdom of Sweden. I wish you a pleasant journey."

When they came to a stop, Aggrey reached into his pocket and pulled out a twenty pound note and gave it to

Per. Sandile remembered that Per was insistent on people paying their way.

"Thank you, Per, for all of your assistance. I wish to see you one day soon in your Kingdom of Sweden."

"Aggrey, I bid you farewell, my dear friend, and God speed."

Aggrey and Per shook hands and gave one another a hug. Per stayed in the taxi whilst Aggrey unloaded Sandile and Nobuhlali's bags. Sandile and Nobuhlali waved at Per from the curb of the street and watched him drive away as their father was getting a trolley for their bags. They made it to their check-in point without incident and within forty-five minutes of arriving got on the plane and were on their way to Sweden.

For the two-hour flight they sat together on the aisle of the airplane with three seats right next to one another. Again, they seldom spoke and, when they did, they spoke in English. They were all still apprehensive because of the experience that they had had in getting to London. But from the experience with Per, the children seemed more relaxed, anticipating that all Swedes they came across would be like Per and spoke openly to one another during the flight, although it was in English.

Aggrey was a bit annoyed with himself. He had not spent enough time with his children, and they seemed to have grown without him. Nobuhlali was mature beyond her age and Sandile did not have anyone aside from his grandmother to speak to him about manhood. He strongly wished that Sandile were more influenced by his Fanti culture from Ghana, but he understood there was nothing he could do about the past and he had to focus on the future.

He looked down at his children and saw two young adults who had accepted how complicated the world was and seemed to be adjusting well to leaving everything they knew behind in order to be with their parents and allow them to do their work. Aggrey made a promise to himself that he would take them both to Accra in Ghana before they returned to South Africa, to meet his father Jonas who was now getting old, so he could see his grandchildren one more time before he passed on. He reached out, rubbed his children's heads and said the Lord's Prayer in silence for his family's safety. God had protected them thus far.

They arrived in Sweden at the end of summer, in August of 1985, one month after the state of emergency had been declared in South Africa. Swedes generally were in a good mood, outgoing and friendly in the summer, and not morose and withdrawn like they were in the winter. They arrived at the best time for the children to make friends at school before the onset of a dark and long winter.

When they arrived at the arrivals area of the airport, they saw the sign Välkommen till Konungariket Sverige [Welcome to the Kingdom of Sweden] and they knew they'd arrived in their new home.

Sandile and Nobuhlali's mother Phumla was awaiting them in the arrivals area. When she saw them, it was as if she had seen them for the first time or she had not been sure if they would arrive safely in Sweden. She broke into tears and ran and hugged and kissed them both on the forehead.

Aggrey was more measured and stood back whilst the children and their mother had their moment. She reached out to him while hugging the children and hugged him as well. He responded by shedding a tear and exclaiming, "God is great!"

They all stood there in an embrace for a couple of moments, relishing being together again and in a safe environment for the whole family. Sandile looked around while in an embrace with his family and could not notice any people of colour. Although he felt safe, the environment suddenly became foreign to him. Because he felt safe, he could not understand the paradox.

From the airport they got into a taxi, which took them to a quaint three-bedroom apartment in the middle of Stockholm in the old town, called Gamla Stan. It would be from there that Sandile and Nobuhlali would learn to walk the Stockholm streets in safety and also make new friends, which would replace some of their feelings of longing for home.

Their parents considered this as a chance for their family to start over again and for them to rediscover their children. Aggrey and Phumla enrolled Sandile and Nobuhlali at the Stockholm International School, where they felt their chances of normalising in a new country would be best optimised. The school taught the students in English and they also had Swedish classes so that the children could pick up the local language. In their flat in Gamla Stan, the children each had their own rooms, which allowed them to develop their sense of self more effectively than the room they'd both shared in their grandmother's three-roomed house in Cofimvaba, where the kitchen was one of the rooms.

The children needed very little time to adjust to Sweden and within a couple of weeks they had made new friends whom they would often invite home after school or would go to their houses without much trepidation. They did not fear the new culture and became increasingly less conscious of the fact that they were amongst the few children of colour within their school.

The children adjusting well to the new culture and country allowed Aggrey and Phumla to focus on their work without worrying too much about the development of their children. They would spend the weekends with some of the African families that had moved to Sweden as a result of colonialism and stayed there, or because of apartheid. They had a melting pot of cultures to be influenced by and that is where Sandile and Nobuhlali would learn the story of a new Africa, one that they were not learning in school.

Shortly after their admission to Stockholm International School, they realised that there were two African stories that were being told: the stories in their educational system and the stories they were being told at home through their family friends. They had to combine these two to make a common story of Africa for themselves.

During one of their family outings, they became friends with a young man of about eleven years old named Simon. Simon was also a student at Stockholm International School. Through him, they realised that the history of Africa that was being taught in their school in their history classes started from the sixteenth century until present. It was not a multidimensional history that took into account the holistic development of Africa but was focused on how Africa developed as a reaction to slavery and colonialism.

It was not until they met Simon that they would begin to consider that Africa had a history that spanned centuries before Christ and that the new African story was emerging on the home front and abroad and was not only to be found in their educational system but at home too.

Simon was an unassuming young man but there was always something strange about him. At school he would be followed around by a bodyguard who was so dark that he had almost a purplish tone about him. Sandile and Nobuhlali wondered on many occasions where such a person could come from and naturally assumed it was West Africa or Ghana, since some of the people from there also had very dark tones like their father. They always assumed that Simon was the child of some dignitary and therefore needed twenty-four-hour protection.

He was naturally very good at basketball since he was very tall and with a physique that gave him advantage on the basketball court. Sandile made friends whilst playing basketball and over time they would become very good friends. He then introduced him to his sister Nobuhlali and they all got along very well.

Having had to move to a new country as a result of apartheid, Sandile and Nobuhlali did not think that in postcolonial Africa there were still other stories that were playing themselves out in the African continent that they were not being taught about in school. It was not until Simon became comfortable with them that he told them that his father was Mr. John Garang, the leader of the Sudanese People's liberation army during Sudan's second civil war.

The Second Sudanese Civil War was a conflict that started in 1983 between the central Sudanese government and the Sudanese People's Liberation Army. Simon and his mother were in hiding in Sweden from the war. The war was largely a continuation of the First Sudanese Civil War of 1955 to 1972. Simon's father Mr. Garang had moved Simon to Sweden with his mother Faeema, because he thought the war in Sudan would be one of the longest civil wars on record in Africa.

Through Simon, Sandile and Nobuhlali would learn a different history of Africa, starting with the Nubians and also their accomplishments in Northern Sudan and ancient Egypt. The stories they learned did not come from their school education but through their childhood friend.

The conflict that was happening in Sudan at the time was also not covered their school education and many of the questions they had about the conflict they would ask their parents or friend Simon or his mother, who was always willing to shed some light on the conflict. It took them a while to adjust to the parallel African narrative when they arrived in Stockholm and gettingt access to the emerging African story would not be through their formal education, but it would be through family and their friend.

It was in informal family settings at many of their parents' friends' houses that they would learn about the emergence of the new Africa that their parents were working towards. A lot of their friends' parents in Stockholm were educated in other countries and wanted to go back to Africa to live and to work. They had somewhat of a global view to the emergence of the new Africa. They also had stories of Africa and its place in the world that went beyond slavery and colonialism and sought to answer the question of what their common heritage was.

Their friends' parents ranged from mathematicians to academics to liberation fighters, but they all concurred that there was a new Africa that was emerging with the new African.

Over some months, Sandile and Nobuhlali became very good friends with Simon. They would play and share stories of their countries together. Sandile and Nobuhlali, when they had learned to trust Simon, also told him about South Africa and the state of emergency and how they had fled South Africa from the security police.

Simon's mother Faeema got on well with their parents and over the coming months they would plan trips together to surrounding Scandinavian countries in order to expose the children to the full culture of Scandinavia.

Things were progressing well. Sandile and Nobuhlali had adjusted to life in Sweden and their parents were getting on well with their work within the small African community that they had discovered in Stockholm. Aggrey and Phumla and Simon's mother trusted the children would be safe on the streets of Stockholm and on many occasions would allow them to travel back and forth to one another's house unaccompanied, albeit with Simon's security guard trailing behind.

They adapted well to the egalitarian nature of school and the other children did not treat them any differently to themselves. They also got on very well with the other children at school. Over time, Sandile and Nobuhlali begun to recognise the spirit of their village Cofimvaba in Sweden's open and kind inhabitants. Everyone seemed to have a culture of looking out for one another and the children were thriving in their new environment. Simon's mother Faeema even enrolled at Stockholm University to study finance and strategy with Phumla.

The families of the children became very close and begun to form an extended family. The children were sharing experiences of the continent together and learning from all the other African families and they were becoming increasingly conscious about the challenges that they faced as young Africans in a foreign land. Although they were young, they understood the complexity of their lives and increasingly became mature and aware of their own Africanness through one another.

The African community in Stockholm was a very small and intimate community composed mainly of academics. They were extremely serious about creating a new generation of conscious young Africans. Sandile, Nobuhlali and Simon were the beneficiaries of this intellectual ambition within the small African community. The other children at Stockholm international school were also very keen to learn as much as they could about the children's African culture whilst at the same time teaching them about Swedish and Scandinavian culture. It was an international school with children from all around Scandinavia and other parts of the world.

Because there were some students there from America, Sandile and Nobuhlali were told by their parents not to speak about the trip to America that they had cancelled, since their parents were somewhat fearful of the long arm of the American government. Sandile and Nobuhlali had become very good at subterfuge and this only fuelled their relationship with Simon who thought that he could learn a lot from them and thoroughly enjoyed their company.

He had also been through trauma in seeing the effects of civil war and leaving his country under a cloud of urgency for his and his mother's life. He identified with Sandile and Nobuhlali to such an extent that he often referred to them as his brother and sister when introducing them to other people.

Although Simon and Nobuhlali were a year apart, with Nobuhlali a year older, she took a liking to him that went beyond the realms of sisterly love. She expressed her love for him by always agreeing with him when he and Sandile got into a disagreement. He also noticed her childish infatuation with him and reciprocated by bringing something to share at school with her during their lunches.

Sandile was not threatened by their relationship and even supported it as it reminded him of his love for Anelisa. However, when Aggrey and Phumla noticed the developing relationship between Simon and Nobuhlali, they stopped letting Simon have sleepovers at their house. Sandile could sleep over at Simon's house but Simon could not spend the nights at his house because of Nobuhlali.

Aggrey and Phumla considered this ban to be appropriate, although they respected and even encouraged Nobuhlali and Simon's relationship. They were living in a time where the children's relationships had been shattered through war and apartheid and what little humanity they found in themselves Aggrey, Phumla and Faeema were willing to allow the children to develop amongst themselves.

Stockholm for the children was a very open society with kind people and this only fuelled the children's curiosity about the new culture, which they were discovering day by day. They made new friends at school and each day they had new and exciting stories to share with their parents. Aggrey was happy that Sandile did not want to grow up as fast as he had grown in Cofimvaba and was no longer preoccupied with manhood. He now had the time to be a child in a safe community that supported his childhood.

It had been months since Sandile had spoken about circumcision and going to the mountains and he was now just focused on having fun and learning from the other children in his school. He had discovered from Simon that it was not common for children to be circumcised when they became adults in Sudan and this gave him some comfort that there was no rush for him to become a man since Simon seemed not to give it too much attention.

Although Sandile and Nobuhlali missed their grandmother Rhundu and would often ask their parents about her, Cofimvaba seemed to be a distant memory and a lifetime ago. Aggrey and Phumla did not take the risk of phoning Rhundu because they knew that the security police were everywhere in South Africa. They could make things very difficult for Rhundu if they knew that she was an accomplice to them leaving the country. However, the security police now had no influence over Aggrey and Phumla's work in Stockholm, or so they thought.

Their feelings of safety in Sweden were, however, about to come to a crashing halt with the assassination of the prime minister Olof Palme some months after their arrival in Sweden.

On Friday, the 28th of 1986, Sandile and Phumla came home to an eerie environment. Their parents were sitting in the TV room holding hands whilst their mother was crying, and their father had his hands over his mouth to cover his shock. The children thought they were watching an adult movie of some sort and did not want to be disturbed, but they caught the news anchor announcing the assassination of the prime minister and that the assassin could be a South African security agent. The state of emergency had followed them to Sweden and Sandile and Nobuhlali were terrified in terms of what this meant for their family.

Within minutes, Stockholm went from being a safe and fulfilling environment for their family to a dangerous place that now filled them with the dread that they had left behind in South Africa. Even the prime minister of Sweden was not safe from the state of emergency at home and the South African security agents. There were suspicions that a South

African intelligence agent had killed the prime minister of Sweden on the streets of Stockholm.

Thoughts of manhood suddenly flooded Sandile's mind again. He thought about his grandmother and that, if he were only a man, he could go back home and protect her. If he were a man, he could protect his family with his father from the South African security agents who had now assassinated the Swedish Prime minister.

Nobuhlali also thought about her grandmother, but her thoughts were on her parents too. She could not bear her family being torn apart by apartheid again since they were so happy in Sweden and her family was together. She thought about what this meant for her family and she panicked and begun to have an anxiety attack.

Her parents were glued to the TV and she was gasping for air. She grabbed Sandile's hand and pointed at her throat with her other hand and her mouth wide open. Sandile was terrified as this had never happened before. Perhaps the security police had poisoned his sister as they had so many other children in his village with their families. Sandile was thrust back to Cofimvaba and his childhood immediately left him. He was now the young man who had travelled from Cofimvaba to London on his own and the child in him was distant memory.

He calmly called out to his parents. "Mama, Tata, I think Nobuhlali has been poisoned. She can't breathe."

His parents jumped to attention and noticed Sandile's serious face. He had the expression of an old man who had been through numerous traumatic life experiences. Aggrey picked Nobuhlali up and laid her on the couch. Phumla had been a nurse before she became a social worker and had seen many anxiety attacks in young people caused by trauma.

"No, my boy, she has not been poisoned; she is having an anxiety attack. It will pass."

Aggrey lay beside Nobuhlali, stroking her head and asking her to take her time breathing and to calm down. She slowly regained her breathing and began to calm down with the loving help of her parents. Phumla noticed that Sandile had taken offense to her addressing him as "my boy" and she was scared for her children, both for Sandile's mental health and for Nobuhlali's physical health.

For a while, the family stood there, over Nobuhlali, whilst she regained her breathing, not saying a word to one another. The whole family had been traumatised by the events of the day and no words could allay their fears about their volatile future.

Phumla stood there staring at her children and she was drawn back to the early eighties when she'd had to do social work in Zimbabwe during the reign of the Gukurahundi. In 1981, North Korean military instructors arrived in Zimbabwe after Prime Minister Robert Mugabe announced that former guerrillas would form a militia to combat "malcontents" who were unleashing a reign of terror in the country. Mugabe signed an agreement with Kim Il Sung of North Korea, which would train and arm this brigade, most of whom were Shona speaking. The brigade, which was called 5 Brigade, became known as the Gukurahundi, a Shona expression meaning "the rain that washes away the chaff". Within weeks of being mobilised in January 1983, the brigade was responsible for the death of 2 000 civilians, most of whom were Ndebele.

Phumla had never witnessed the effects of ethnic cleansing before and for the first time she saw the trauma that civil conflict had on children. She was seeing the same effects on her children of physical stress. They looked like they had aged a number of decades within a space of a short time. During the reign of the Gukurahundi, Ndebele people were being killed en masse and, on many occasions, she saw pregnant women who had been shot in the stomach or who had had their babies cut out their stomach by the brigade.

There were numerous disappearances of entire families, which were found later in mass graves with one to twelve people being buried in one grave. During her stint in Zimbabwe, she was brought to the brink of a mental breakdown by what she saw, with black people killing their own under the proposition that some people belonged to a different tribe or different ethnic group.

In the middle of 1983, she then decided to work with an American NGO to bring financial and material relief to those who had been affected by the Gukurahundi. However, she soon learned that the American NGOs she was working with were using their presence in Zimbabwe to spy on the government on behalf of the South African government. Aside from a public show of support for those Ndebele families who were affected, the American NGOs had rather nefarious reasons for being in Zimbabwe.

She then met some Chinese companies that had become involved in Zimbabwe in gold and diamond extraction, and they'd sponsored her to go to China to further her studies before she went to Sweden to continue her studies and be with her family. The Chinese companies that were in Zimbabwe at the time were careful not to take political stances in the country, but they sought to meet their commercial and social obligations to the country by training capable Africans in China, and giving them the tools to survive on a complex continent.

Whilst doing social work in Zimbabwe, she had used the cover to her family that she was working in East London as a social worker. Only her husband Aggrey and her mother Rhundu knew she was assisting the dissidents in Zimbabwe. The experience in Zimbabwe allowed Phumla to learn that the challenges facing the African were not only oppression from white people, but also oppression from their own black people. Something had to be done. In China, she found a group of radical Africans who were working on a new plan for Africa's development known as NEPAD.

It was then that she had roped her husband Aggrey into her work. He would work on the ground with the trade unions in South Africa, gathering intel on what he considered the future of Africa would be like beyond colonialism and apartheid. She had worked with the African academics she had met in China to put together the NEPAD document with the experiences of her husband on the ground.

Her thoughts were brought crashing back into the room when Sandile yelled out. "Tata, Mama, I think I am ready to be a man now. Please take me to the hospital now to be circumcised!"

Phumla wanted to say no immediately, but she saw that Aggrey was seriously considering the idea as he had his right hand on his cheek whilst caressing Nobuhlali's forehead with the other. Nobuhlali was very upset about what had just happened with the Swedish prime minister and the supposed South African agent. She thought surely they would come after her family next and it was time for Sandile to become a man. She concurred with Sandile.

"Yes, Sandile, I also think it is time you became a man so that there are two men in the house instead of one to protect our family."

Phumla broke into tears as she realised she was the only one in the family who was not ready for her eleven-year-old son to grow up. She wanted him to be a child in Sweden just for a bit longer, even it were only for a couple more days. She was just not ready to give him up to manhood.

Aggrey, on the other hand, thought that being in Sweden had allowed the children to buy into a fantasy that the world was a safe and nurturing place and that shielded them from the realities on their continent. The peaceful community in Sweden was not going to do them any favours.

Aggrey had served in the military in Ghana before pursuing his studies. All of a sudden, he was that military man again, and he became rather militant and resolute. "I will call Karolinska University Hospital today and see if they can do the procedure as a matter of urgency this week. It's okay. Instead of going to the mountain, Sandile will spend the next month in his room healing and I will tell him what is required of manhood according to Fanti culture."

Everyone remained frozen after Aggrey spoke. The assassination of the prime minister had also had an effect on him. He wanted to protect his family at all costs and not shield them from the grim reality of the events of the day. The faster they all accepted the reality that life was unkind, the better prepared they would be for the future. He walked towards the phone at the front door entrance of the flat and called the Karolinska Hospital. Within five minutes, he had organised a date for Sandile to be admitted. The family all stayed quiet during the phone call, with each one trying to follow the conversation he was having on the phone.

"I told them it was an emergency and they have an opening tonight for the procedure. Sandile, we will leave the house in an hour. Please get yourself ready."

It was mid-afternoon. The doctor had told Aggrey that Sandile would have to be in the hospital two hours early in order to be prepared for the procedure. Sandile scurried to his room and began packing an overnight bag for his stay at the hospital. Phumla was still in shock over her husband's decision. This was the first time he had made a decision without consulting her, but she knew this situation required resolute leadership. She did not harbour a grudge against him for it and respected his decision. She knew he was acting in the best interests of the family.

Aggrey waited for Sandile at the kitchen table on his own whilst sipping slowly on a cup of coffee he had prepared. Phumla lay with Nobuhlali on the couch as they comforted one another, trying to make the moment less traumatic than it was. They both knew things had changed in the family. Life was not going to be the same again and their father would never let his guard down again, even if they were going to spend a couple more years in Sweden.

Within an hour, Sandile was ready with his overnight bag and his toiletries. To Phumla, the hour seemed like less than a minute. Her mind was still in Zimbabwe, thinking of the effects of the Gukurahundi on young children and their families. She wanted to protect her family and she knew at this moment the best way to do that was to be supportive of her husband's decision. When Sandile was ready, he went to stand at the front door. All he could see on his mother's face in the TV room was a look of despair, but she was trying to be strong for her family. She wiped the tears from her face and continued with her wet hands to rub Nobuhlali's head and comfort her.

Aggrey stood up from the dining table in the kitchen and, without saying a word to his wife and daughter, walked out of the house and he and Sandile were off to Karolinska University Hospital. A mother had said goodbye to her son's innocence in silence. The trauma of the moment would not rob Phumla of her family's innocence. She was more resolute on that day to provide her children an upbringing that was deserving of their kindness and joy for life that they had experienced in their first few months in Sweden.

For the rest of the evening, Phumla and Nobuhlali lay on the couch together, not saying a word. They fell asleep on the couch until the next morning, not knowing when Sandile would return a man.

The next morning at five, Aggrey brought Sandile home from the hospital. Phumla and Nobuhlali were still sleeping on the couch and did not see them walk in. For the next month, they would not be allowed to speak to or see Sandile, as his father Aggrey confined him to his room for the rights of passage. He would make Sandile breakfast in the morning, followed by a talk for an hour and, at night was dinner, followed by another talk for an hour.

This went on for a month, with Aggrey never discussing with Phumla or Nobuhlali what he and Sandile had spoken about. After a month, Sandile came out of his room and for the first time had dinner with the family. He did not speak other than to greet his mother and sister and occasionally asking them to pass him some food on the dinner table.

His mother was somewhat relieved because he seemed to have the look of a child again and not some old man, like on the day he'd left to the hospital with his father. She knew that something had gone right with her husband's talks with him, and her husband had managed to save their son's innocence, although he never discussed what he and Sandile had talked about during that month.

Nobuhlali was not quite sure how to address her brother since he'd become a man, and she took her time observing him and trying to get to know him again. He could see that she was apprehensive to address him and so he reached out to his sister. This was to show her that manhood was not some incomprehensible personal path but was an increase in one's proximity to one's family, as his father had told him over and over in his time alone in his room.

"So, how is Simon?"

She was somewhat relieved that she could talk to her brother again. She noticed something had changed in his tone. He was no longer the hesitant young brother that she had known. He carried their father's confidence, and he was rather resolute in his speech. But his tone also had an element of respect for her, as his older sister. She looked at him for a moment, to take it all in, before she responded.

"Oh, you know Simon, he is fine and still telling me stories about his home. I know so much about Sudan now. But don't worry, he spoke to your teachers and got all of your homework for you so you will not be left behind in class."

Phumla was not quite sure if she should hug Sandile or keep her distance. She was still not sure how he interpreted his manhood. To her surprise, he reached out to her, gave her a kiss on the cheek as he had seen his father do on so many occasions, followed by a hug.

The whole family was relieved that Sandile had not lost his childhood and, although he was now a man, he was still a son to his mother and a younger brother to his sister. In Sandile's mind, manhood was about assisting his father to take care of his family. Over the next five years in Sweden, Sandile grew very close to his mother and sister and became increasingly protective over them with age.

His relationship with Simon also took an adult tone, as they would often do things together as young men without his sister Nobuhlali. Her relationship with Simon also grew and with time they became more intellectually and emotionally intimate with one another, always making sure to respect the boundaries that their parents had set for them.

As their parents learned, with Phumla achieving a PhD in finance and Simon's mother Faeema a Master's in finance, so the children grew within their proximity to Africa. Through their parents they understood more clearly the challenges that the continent faced and what level of conscientisation they had to achieve as young Africans in Sweden. It took a couple of years after the death of Olof Palme to normalise within the African community.

But slowly things did go back to normal. The community went from being insular and protective after his death to slowly engaging in the Swedish way of life again after a couple of years. The community was still guarded.

Sunday the 11th of February 1990 was a special day for the African community in Stockholm, especially Aggrey and Phumla. Nelson Mandela was released from prison after twenty-seven years of imprisonment by the apartheid government. There were celebrations at people's houses all over Stockholm within the small African community. South Africa was the last African state to achieve independence. People within the country had made it ungovernable with the support of the African diaspora outside of the country.

By the 90s, times seemed to have changed and Sandile's family could finally go back home and he would see Rhundu and Anelisa again. Although Sandile and Nobuhlali would be leaving their friend Simon behind in Stockholm, leaving

Sweden and their new-found community, they still had a yearning for their village of Cofimvaba.

Aggrey and Phumla were, however, a bit measured and curbed the children's childish exuberance. They told the children that things in South Africa were still too volatile for them to return. Negotiations for a new constitution were taking place, but the old security apparatus was still at work with many people dying in KwaZulu-Natal and people being arrested in urban South Africa for conspiring with the apartheid government and being brought in front of the Truth and Reconciliation Commission. It was too early to go back to South Africa as things were still volatile. They concurred with the excitement of the children and decided that it was time to go back to the continent to add to the new-found transformative energy that had been released at the release of Nelson Mandela.

Aggrey and Phumla accepted jobs with the International Monetary Fund (IMF) and World Bank. Aggrey would put together scenarios on the future of investment opportunities for the IMF in sub-Saharan Africa, based in Nairobi, Kenya. Phumla got a job with the World Bank, working with women empowerment in business, also based in Nairobi. Although these were American agencies that Phumla and Aggrey would be working for, they both agreed that times had changed and the US could be a good development partner for Africa going forward.

Simon's mother also decided to move to Kenya with Simon so she could be closer her husband's movement in Sudan and be of support to him during the war. Within a month of the release of Nelson Mandela, both families were on their way back to the mother continent. Aggrey and Phumla would, however, make their return to the continent via Accra, Ghana, so that the children could meet their grandfather Jonas. Aggrey and Phumla told the children that the time to contact Rhundu directly was still not right, since things were still not stable in South Africa.

Over the years, they had managed to keep in touch with her through letters that they addressed to Mr. Dabula at Village School so that the security police would not be able to trace their whereabouts. She had told them how Cofimvaba had changed over the last five years since they had been out of the country. It now had a shopping mall and people from surrounding villages came to do their shopping in Cofimvaba. Cofimvaba was now a melting pot of ideas and people were more positive about the country than ever.

She told them that, although Nelson Mandela had been released, there was still a fear of the security police, who were trying to undermine the negotiations in the country led by Nelson Mandela and his African National Congress. People were still disappearing and there were unexplained detentions and unexplained deaths.

She concurred with Sandile and Nobuhlali's mother and father that the time to come back to South Africa was still not right and they should stay abroad for a while. She told them how she prayed for them and that she hoped that God protected them. In her letters, she still addressed Sandile as inkwenkwe, although he was circumcised. He did not seem to mind, however, as his grandmother's safety was more important to him than his manhood.

Since he had been circumcised, manhood did not seem to play that much of a role for him in his life. Perhaps it was the conversations during his month of healing that pacified some ideas around manhood, or it was life and growing up, or a mixture of the two. Sandile's main preoccupation with age was the safety of his family and their happiness.

Lastly, Rhundu told them that Anelisa was also doing fine and she had become a beautiful young woman and that she feared for her well-being as all the men in the village were making advances on her.

She had done as Sandile had wanted to suggest to her some years ago and had sent her to the Catholic boarding school that Nobuhlali had attended to keep her out of harm's way. This made Sandile a bit more settled and his urgency to get back to his village was somewhat abated.

She wished them well on their trip to Ghana and their move to Nairobi, and asked Nobuhlali to assist her mother to take care of the family and for Sandile to be a partner with his father in protecting the family.

She was happy that they had been treated so well in the Kingdom of Sweden.

6

In the last letter from Rhundu, which the children received via Mr. Dabula, Rhundu wrote them a letter which she titled *Uhuru (Freedom); The rise of the new African*. She insisted that they should wait until they were on the airplane on their way to their first African stop in Ghana before going to their final destination in Kenya, to read the contents of the letter. She thought it would prepare them for their move to Africa.

When Sandile and Nobuhlali got on the plane with their parents on their way to a stopover in Frankfurt, then Ghana, they were in eager anticipation of the contents of the last letter their grandmother had sent them. She always had words of wisdom well beyond her years and the children learned a lot about their continent from her letters.

They took their seats on the airplane and waited for the plane to take off before they opened the letter. When the plane got to cruising altitude, they opened the envelope to take out the letter that was to be shared amongst themselves. Nobuhlali read the contents of the letter out loud, since her written and spoken English were still better than Sandile's. The letter read:

My dear my grandchildren, Nobuhlali and Sandile

It has been five years since we have seen one another. Your parents have told me that you have grown into responsible young adults and that makes my heart glad. From the correspondence I have received from you, I can tell you have grown and your hunger for Africa has accompanied that growth. I can say I am proud of that development. I know you have learned a lot in Sweden about the world and in particular Africa from the small African community there, but I would like to complement that learning with some of the assessments I have made whilst living on the continent for the last five years. These will add to the body of knowledge you have on Africa.

It is my wish that this letter will prepare you again to live on the African continent and to thrive when you get to your final destination, Kenya, as young Africans. I will try and be brief, but the contents of this letter must be told to you before your arrival so that you are well informed about some of the challenges on the continent.

In my view, Africa in the next hundred years can be any kind of society that it applies its will and effort to with children such as yourselves, who have seen the world. We don't have to be limited through current events in the kind of Africa that we would like to see in the future, and scenarios that we design don't have to be limited to how current events will shape future events. I have often said this to your father in his work with

African scenarios and your mother with her academic work on Africa.

In focusing on the future, Africa should be able to retell its story with ambitious thinking for the future that we would like to design for the kind of Africa we would like to live in. Your father's scenarios on many occasions have resonated with the kind of Africa that I see in the future and I applaud his work. The limitations of the mind are where innovation should begin and it should end where ambition charts the course for a more future-focused African continent.

Your mother has reminded me on many occasions through her studies that this is how great and innovative societies have emerged – by creating human confidence in the belief that the future can be better and can better be designed to meet the needs of complex societies. Your mother has also seen during her studies that Africa needs to start forming its own theories of the past, present and future and needs to transform itself into a knowledge economy.

There are many interventions that need to be made on the African continent in order to be able to do this and that is through engaging legacy institutions and telling a different story of the future. Legacy institutions, which I consider myself to be part of, provide the basis and grounding for the young to be able to form alternative futures for a more complex and innovative African continent. In providing this basis for innovation, this does not mean that younger generations such as yours should not challenge the status quo of legacy institutions. Your future generation of young Africans should have a determined spirit that fosters an appreciation of legacy institutions whilst at the same time answering the question of, "What different thinking can add to the accomplishments of your forefathers?"

Your generation, as the beneficiaries of legacy institutions in South Africa and Africa alike, should seek a deeper understanding of the foundations of those legacy institutions in order to further entrench positive and constructive futures of a continent. My generation, as a living legacy institution, should continue to exist in society by being fuelled by the energy of your generation of young Africans, with your ideas and ambitions.

Legacy institutions such as myself have a strong role to play in the future of generations to come. The role for legacy institutions in the future will not exist organically or simply by communal memory but will develop through evolving to recreate themselves to meet new challenges of your future generations.

Although legacy institutions like myself represent the foundations of the past, they must be re-informed through your young voices on the trajectory of the future that you can positively shape for coming generations. Africa itself is a legacy institution for our generation that we have to deal with in our own unique ways and this is where the new African in your generation is to emerge in new approaches to Africa's old problems. The neo-colonial classical approaches to the African story have yielded very few results in terms of generating a new continental consciousness.

I would argue that in Africa there is the emergence of a new African that has a new collective consciousness in how *they engage Africa as a legacy institution. This new African, being your generation, has a greater sense of time with regards to the development of the African continent as a legacy institution which dates back to the ancient Nubians and the ancient Egyptians - all the way to 300*BC.

The point of departure for the new African in your generation is not with the landing of the European colonialists in Africa, but begins three centuries before Christ and the modern bible. It is a story of an innovative and progressive Africa, which went through a renaissance that can be realised again in the not-so-distant future in Africa. This is what in essence reinforces authentic consciousness for the new Africa in your generation, based on a historical shared African heritage.

From what you told me of your discussions with your friend Simon, you both understand that we as Africans come from an era of great African kings and queens and are of a society and legacy that was born many years before Christ. We were accomplished mathematicians, scientists and philosophers before the common era of man. It is a difficult proposition, but I would like to suggest that people of African descent have had their renaissance before in Ancient Northern Sudan in an area called Nubia and in lower Egypt and northern Sudan, and that Africans must reawaken the spirit of that historical renaissance for this new millennium.

Nubia was home to some of Africa's earliest kingdoms. Monuments still stand – in modern Egypt and Sudan – at the sites where Nubian rulers built cities, temples and royal pyramids. Nubia is a region along the Nile River, located in what is today northern Sudan and southern Egypt. It was one of the earliest civilisations of ancient north-eastern Africa, with a history that can be traced from at least 3 000BCE onward, and was home to one of the African empires.

There is a new search, now more than ever, for the African story with African images, especially for your generation. We have had many liberation movements in Africa to liberate the African from social, economic and political systems that sought to subjugate the African soul and mind. We are going through a twentieth century marked by the overwhelming belief, on a global scale, that the African must be an equal participant in the global order. Your generation is now left with the task of redefining the African story and also its origins within a global system.

The great questions that we Africans must answer are: what is our common and mutual heritage? How can we also leverage the experiences of our ancestors dating back to ancient Nubia to foster the kind of societies that we would like to develop in the upcoming millennia? What is the emerging African story and how can we inculcate the learning of the past to our children and our children's children? Also, how do we retune the way in which we educate our youth so that it will motivate a new-found sense of Africanism within them?

As you know, children, our family is complex and we have lived through some difficult times. I also spent some time in Kenya, where your final destination will be, on holiday. Whilst visiting in Kenya, I discovered some intellectual freedoms that we take for granted in South Africa, and it was an accepted norm that Kenya was an African country with African ideals and values. There was a wonderful energy about Kenya where I felt free to pursue the questions I had about my African-ness. I thought then, and I still do think now, that in order for Africa to begin to channel its new narrative it has to combine both the formal and informal narrative of Africa that is playing itself out on the African continent, whilst making the new African beyond colour and class.

South Africa is an African state on the continent of Africa and has much to learn from the other African nations on the continent. South Africa has political lessons of responsible governance to learn from Africa. The lessons of colonialism and what became of some African states post-colonialism must be a source of wealth for South Africa in these trying times during our transition to a new constitution. This is not only in how to develop good governance but also how to develop a market system that is driven by the needs of the entire population and not just an elite few.

In many African nations there has been the birth of a predatory elite after liberation. This predatory elite has amassed huge fortunes for themselves at the expense of development in some African countries. This elite also makes sure there is no trickle-down version of the free market to those who are less fortunate and does not actively push for the creation of a viable and conscious middle class. This elite maintains the old status quo of colonial masters of development and prosperity for a few. South Africa is also in danger of this phenomenon of developing a predatory elite if it is not careful. No African country is immune to poor governance.

The African condition is unique because organic development in Africa was disrupted by years of slavery, colonialism and apartheid, which impeded the unleashing of African human potential towards its own development agenda. This means both South Africa and Africa have to be dynamic in how they develop the emergence of the new African of your generation in the development agenda. Freedom entails that people are also spiritually and intellectually free, in order for societies to be able to progress.

No amount of money or financial success can bring about an intellectual and spiritual freedom. Spiritual freedom entails being grounded in the values of pan Africanism in that we are all, as African states, in this game of development together. Spiritual freedom could also be what we South Africans relate to as ubuntu: "I am because we are, and when I dehumanise you I dehumanise myself".

Secondly, there is intellectual freedom that is to be guaranteed by the right to education. Education is not limited to formal education but can also be inclusive of the informal in indigenous educational practices through indigenous languages of African nations. There is a lot of value to be unleashed in indigenous African education that is not currently being used. African nations should start to rely more on indigenous education to drive local growth, such as in Uganda where indigenous education is the norm.

It is through spiritual and intellectual freedom that the new African of your generation is going to drive the trajectory of the African continent. It is possible to teach children such as yourselves from a young age to have a sense of meaning in their nation and redefine the way that you would like to participate in your societies by having curricula that are aimed at rebuilding your souls. Indigenous education will go a long way in increasing your confidence as African children when you are older and are market participants. You will be able to engage the market with indigenous African world views.

The new African of your generation is globally complex whilst at the same time being able to deal with the local realities it finds itself in. The new African is the driver for a new consciousness in a market system that serves the needs of all Africans and not just a limited few. The new African in your generation is the basis for a new kind of indigenous development that we need to start seeing across the African continent. The new African of your generation is conscious that philosophy drives change. The new African is specific about what it means to be an African in this new century. It is about accepting the limitations of the past and what has happened to Africa, whilst using those experiences of our forefathers to drive the change we need and want in our societies.

We need the emergence of a new kind of African in your generation who is able to drive the trajectory of this continent towards states that are inclusive with responsible and transparent governance. Africa is not the Dark Continent it used to once be and is now becoming a beacon of hope.

It is in unleashing the potential of the youth that Africa can start to come up with new and innovative ideas around development. Forty years of independence in Africa have led to the emergence of the New African in your generation, which seeks to retell the African narrative in a new way, whilst being cognisant of our forefather's contribution to the continent and the sacrifices that were made by a generation in transition. It is on the backbone of the ones who have come before us in the African liberation movements that the new African of your generation is beginning to emerge and change the terms of engagement for the African continent. It is in response to African history that the new African of your generation is cascading the new African narrative across borders with the African diaspora being some of the staunchest proponents of the new African worldview.

Finally, my grandchildren, in conclusion. As I said at the beginning of this letter, the new African of your generation's sense of time is not only to be found within the present or the last four centuries of African recorded subjugation. The new African's sense of time is three thousand or more years before the birth of Jesus Christ. It is biblical in nature, based on researched history of the contribution of the African man and woman to contemporary history. It is a sense of time when Africans had great and innovative societies from the Nubians to the Ancient Egyptians where the African way of life prospered. It a sense of time that allows the African of your generation to see a sense of historical achievement in its past civilisations.

This sense of time allows the young African of your generation to find their place within the past and present annals of history as being contributors to the advancement of man. With a sense of time, the new African of your generation can understand the new narrative of Africa, within an intellectual proximity to African historical achievement in the building of the great pyramids and also the contribution of philosophy, mathematics and medicine to ancient Greece and Rome. It is an intellectual proximity to an African renaissance age that some predict will return once again.

The twentieth century is the rebirth of the African age with the African Renaissance fast approaching. The African Renaissance is the concept that African people and nations shall overcome the current challenges confronting the continent and achieve cultural, scientific and economic renewal. We cannot be stuck in a collective memory that only discusses the difficult paths from the sixteenth century to the integration of the African within the present global socioeconomic order.

Your generation's proximity to a new sense of time should compel you to search a past of African greatness that is documented and also to retell that historical narrative in your own indigenous ways. The African renaissance for the new African has happened before and, through a new collective memory, your generation can give birth to it once again in the present. It is in developing the narrative of the new African that Africa can give birth to its renaissance and forge a new narrative towards the new millennium.

Uhuru, my grandchildren.

When Sandile and Nobuhlali had read the contents of the letter from their grandmother they both looked at one another mischievously and smiled and yelled out, "Uhuru".

Some of the passengers in the plane tried to look over the seats to see what the commotion was but there was nothing to observe; just two happy children. The children were just being children and were showing that they understood their grandmother's message to them in a childish manner. They folded the pages of the letter and gave it to their mother. Their mother over the years had become the record keeper of their correspondence with their grandmother, and they trusted that she would file all their correspondence in a safe place.

She had also become accustomed to the long letters her mother Rhundu would write. She had an ability in her letters to make the reader feel like they were with her as she was writing her letters. She knew how to infuse each letter she wrote to the children with her soul so that they would never forget where they came from and also so that they would be informed of their continent. She was another part of their children's education about Africa that Phumla had grown to appreciate and love. Her children always beamed with love and adoration when they read through their grandmother's letters.

Aggrey referred to Rhundu's letters to the children as their indigenous education. Aggrey could not wait for the children to meet his father Jonas in Accra. He strongly felt that it he would add a new dimension to the children's indigenous education, as he had learned so much from his father as a child growing up there. It was his father who had motivated him to go and teach in South Africa during apartheid because he thought that Aggrey's intellect was needed mostly there, where the country was still fighting for its independence. According to his father Aggrey would be able to bring the Ghanaian liberation movement experience to his students, for them to apply some of his learning.

Aggrey's father was correct and many of Aggrey's students went on to be community leaders and senior political activists who were now within the African National Congress – the ANC – which was negotiating for a new constitution in South Africa. Aggrey's father had never met the children, as Aggrey had not wanted to take the risk of travelling out of South Africa with his children before they moved to Sweden in case he was arrested on his return for political activism. Also, ever since the coup d'état in 1979 in Ghana, Aggrey was a bit unsure if he should return to Ghana as many academics he knew had fled the military leader Jerry Rawlings.

According to history, Rawlings attempted a coup d'état on the 15th of May 1979, leading a group of military personnel in a coup attempt on General Fred Akuffo, which resulted in him being arrested, imprisoned and facing a death sentence. However, a speech he gave during his trial resonated with a large section of the public, which rose up in his defence.

Consequently, on the 4th of June, soldiers sympathetic to his motivations broke him out of jail, and he led a revolt of both the military and civilians, which overthrew General Akuffo and the Supreme Military Council, effectively leaving him in charge. Rawlings and the soldiers around him formed the Armed Forces Revolutionary Council (AFRC) and conducted what it termed a "housecleaning exercise", the aim of which was to purge Ghanaian society of all the corruption and social injustices that they perceived to be at the root of their coup d'état. He took political power in Ghana in 1981 as the Chairman of the Provisional National Defence council and became president of the Republic of Ghana.

In Aggrey's mind, Africa in its entirety was in difficult times. He was cautiously optimistic about the fortunes of Africa, unlike Rhundu who was thoroughly convinced that the new generation would usher in a new African age. This is why he loved working on his scenarios so much, because they allowed him to envision a better Africa for his children. It was an Africa at peace with itself and with responsible governance, which accepted its intellectuals' contributions to the national dialogue.

He did not know what to expect when they landed in Ghana because his father was not a good communicator, but he got the impression that his father also wanted to shield him from what was going on at home. To his father, he would always be his little boy, no matter how old he got. Aggrey's mother had passed away when he was born. His father raised him as an only child. He knew how difficult things could be as an only child and therefore decided to have two children of his own, not so far apart, so that they would not be lonely.

His father was a military man and very strict and so Aggrey had been taught to always be mild mannered and never give too much away to others about himself. It is this predisposition that he also tried to inculcate into his family. His family over the years had learned to love and rely on one another through all difficulty and never approached outsiders about their problems. Rhundu had loved Aggrey from the first time she met him, because he was so responsible around her daughter Phumla and she could see he wanted nothing but the best for her and their union. To his children, Aggrey was like his father, loving but stern, and he had a predictable nature about him. Phumla and the children knew what to expect from him. He was a man for all seasons and a loving father and husband.

The family had a two-hour stopover in Frankfurt, Germany, on their way to Ghana from Stockholm in Sweden. The weather was miserable. It was overcast with slushy brown snow all over the tarmac. It was not a far distant memory from Stockholm which, when they'd left, was very cold with weather still in the minuses. Aggrey assured the children that they need not worry about the weather in Ghana. It was the rainy season now and the weather would be humid and warm and they need not concern themselves about having endless layers of clothes to ward off the cold.

The rainy season in Accra was from March to about June. Although it rained a lot, it was still very hot, reaching temperatures of about forty degrees Celsius, which to Aggrey was very hot. Over the years he had become accustomed to the milder weather in South Africa, which usually does not get too hot or too cold, with periods of drought in between.

The children wanted to walk around the airport. Aggrey thought to himself he did not mind as times were changing in South Africa and he did not fear for the safety of the children on their walkabout. He also did not anticipate they would find anything worth talking about at Frankfurt airport. To him the architecture of the building was dry and mechanical and did not lend itself to children extracting any level of enjoyment from it. Nevertheless, the children found things to see at the airport, from the train station below the airport to the numerous options in the shops, where they bought items that would remind them of Europe when they were in Africa, like T-shirts with the word Frankfurt on them.

The family did not have the time to go out into the city to see the local sights, but Aggrey assured them that on their next trip to Europe they would spend more time in Germany and see some of the cities like Berlin and Munich. Aggrey told his family of his fascination with Germany and its ability to always make remarkable comebacks after the first and second World Wars.

He told them how he wished that some African states had just a small part of the potential of Germany and they would be very developed today. He told the children that Ghana became independent the same year as South Korea in 1957. However, South Korea had used their independence to develop at a much faster pace than Ghana and they were now a second world country on their way to being a first world nation. Ghana was still struggling with being an underdeveloped third world nation.

His history lesson almost caused the family to miss their flight. They were very engrossed in Aggrey's story but they managed to make the boarding time and got on their flight to Accra. The flight from Frankfurt to Accra was about six hours, which meant the family would have the time to prepare for the hot weather in Ghana. The children were looking forward to meeting their grandfather Jonas for the first time. They'd also bought him some presents from Sweden. These were Swedith glass art pieces called Kosta Boda.

For the first time in years, on the plane they were in an environment where there were more people of colour than there were white people. Although for Aggrey and Phumla there was no cultural disorientation, they could tell that the children were having a difficult time adjusting. For the last five years they had been in Sweden where they were the minority in society. They were now in an environment where people who looked like them were the majority. They seemed somewhat disorientated, but Aggrey and Phumla knew they would adjust quickly, before they landed in Ghana, to their new cultural environment.

Simon's mother Faeema had told them that she would follow them to Kenya after their trip to Ghana, arriving shortly after their arrival there. She gave them her new details for Kenya shortly before they left. She had decided to start her return trip in Sudan, where she would meet her husband, the leader of the Sudanese liberation army John Garang, in a secret location before proceeding to Nairobi. Simon's father had not seen his son in five years, and he was insistent that he see his son as soon as he arrived on the continent.

Faeema did not want to separate the children as they had spent most of their formative years together in Sweden evolving from being children to young adults in their teens.

She was insistent that her child would grow up with his childhood friends so that, no matter what challenges life brought him, he would always have a support system of friends he had grown up with to rely on. Because Simon was an only child, she thought he could learn a lot of lessons from Sandile and Phumla, about being able to compromise and get on with other children his age.

Aggrey seldom worried about Nobuhlali because her mother was a strong support system for her, but he often had moments of doubt about Sandile's personal development as a young man. Ever since he'd been circumcised, he seemed to have left his obsession with manhood behind. He no longer spoke about manhood with as much conviction as he'd used to and didn't want to do things that were beyond his age. After the circumcision event he seemed to have settled into his childhood and young adult life very well. He was mature and responsible beyond his age and that was something that made Aggrey very proud.

Initially, when he had taken Sandile to the hospital to get circumcised, he'd thought that would cause a divide between his family and the boy, and he would have some unrealistic expectations of manhood. However, Sandile had adjusted very well, and he had become more himself after the circumcision. He had grown very close to his mother and sister and become increasingly protective over them with time.

Aggrey's relationship with Sandile had also developed and he no longer addressed him as inkwenkwe or boy and they had an egalitarian relationship. Sweden had rubbed off on him and he looked at all his family members as equals to himself and treated them as such. He knew that the law of Jante would follow his family to Africa and he hoped that it would not cause cultural conflicts for his children and wife that they could not manage.

On the plane to Ghana, they spoke, ate and reminisced about their time in Sweden. The children asked Aggrey and Phumla numerous questions about what Ghana and Kenya were like, as they had never been to any other African countries before. Aggrey and Phumla did the best they could to prepare them. They spoke to them about the liberation movements in Africa and African nationalism and its roots and how it represented the collective interest of a unified Africa. They spoke about Ghanaian and Kenyan liberation from colonialism and the paradoxes of African governments.

Phumla, when she saw that the children were eager to understand Africa, also told of the Gukurahundi massacres in Zimbabwe in the early eighties and her experiences there on the ground. They did not want to scare the children about African governance and they also reflected on some of the positive points about the African continent and spoke about the cultural dynamism of the African people.

Phumla mentioned a fact that Aggrey had not known, in that there were more pyramids in Sudan that they were in Egypt. She described Nubian civilisation of northern Sudan for the children and Aggrey and told them how they were the foundations for Egyptian culture and scientific development.

The children were reminded of their friend Simon who on so many occasions had spoken about Nubian culture in northern Sudan with such conviction. He had told them numerous stories of the glory days in 3 000BCE of African civilisations where Africans were innovative and excelled in the sciences.

Time seemed to pass by quickly and before they were aware of it there was an announcement from the cockpit that the plane had started its descent. They were thirty minutes from landing in Accra. Sandile was sitting by the window. He looked down from his window seat to see if he could get a nice view of Accra. All he could see was lush green vegetation. It reminded him of the Swedish forests and a statistic he had learned in school.

In his school, they had taught the children about environmental conservation and that Sweden was amongst the few countries that planted more trees than it cut down. He thought how strange that it was that he was now arriving on the African continent, but he still would not be able to see his grandmother Rhundu and Anelisa for some years to come. He missed them dearly, but the years had given him tools to abate his longing for them. He missed their kindness and especially Anelisa's caring nature.

He had thought about her over the years and what she would look like now that she was older. On many occasions he had played out various conversations that they would have about his trip overseas and the experiences that they'd both had whilst apart. He still had not kissed a girl yet, as he was saving his manhood for Anelisa. Perhaps his vision of being with her was what had pacified his once militant views and childish exuberance about manhood. He no longer considered the act of circumcision so important and over the years it had lost its appeal to him as a right of passage to manhood. The event had come and gone and without him feeling like he had crossed any great hurdle. He had less skin on his penis, but he felt the same.

The conversations with his father during his month of healing from his circumcision had brought clarity for him that the most important thing in life was those you loved, and caring for and nurturing them. The dream that he'd once had about Anelisa being pregnant on his arrival to his village had lost its lustre over the years. He thought it was just that, a dream, and not a sign of things to come. A part of him hoped that, if he had spent all these years to be with her, then surely she had done the same. His fondness for her memory seemed to grow year by year. He was now thinking of Anelisa as a young man would think of a young lady. He no longer imagined her as just a sister, but there were new feelings, which were growing in his heart for her, which he still was battling to deal with.

He had never had these feelings for anyone before and he made a personal commitment that at some stage he would discuss them with his father, Aggrey. He would be able to shed light on them for him since he had been married to his mother Phumla for so long and he had dealt with them for her at some point in their lives.

His sister Nobuhlali was, on the other hand, always secretive about her feelings for Simon and did not discuss them with anyone, not even her mother. It was the kind of person that she was. She was insular and kept everything to herself – both her joys and her suffering.

Her parents assumed she had learned those habits from her grandmother Rhundu. Rhundu's husband Fana, their grandfather, had been arrested in the sixties, during the height of the liberation campaign. He'd died in detention and she seldom spoke about him to her grandchildren. She suffered alone over the years and had found a way to abate her suffering through the joys of her grandchildren. She put all of her focus on them and their well-being as children.

She would only mention their grandfather in passing when she was speaking about the old days. She never told them any great detail about him, except that he was charismatic, and he liked the ladies. Phumla was their only child. Rhundu had taken all of the love she had reserved for her husband Fana and directed it at Phumla's upbringing and her grandchildren. She was strong and a staunch charismatic Methodist Christian woman, but she was also loving and patient with those she loved. She was a pillar of strength within her community and she often helped those in need.

In Cofimvaba, she was known as a lady of God, since she had built the local church in her village with her own money, for the community to gather and pray in. On matters of importance relating to the village of Cofimvaba, the mayor would often consult her before making a decision.

All these personal traits of their grandmother were also personified within Nobuhlali. Her personality over the years had grown to resemble Rhundu more than it did her mother Phumla. Sandile always thought that is why they got along so well as equals, because they were so different. Nobuhlali, however, still played the role of respectful daughter with her mother when the moment demanded it and there were no unhealthy paradoxes between them. However, there was the rare occasion when Nobuhlali would play a motherly role over her mother, especially when she wanted to know about Sandile and his well-being.

Phumla was a person who strongly believed in gender roles, although she also held strong views about male and female equality on the home front. She believed men and woman were equal but different.

THE PLANE LANDED comfortably and quickly came to a standstill. A small truck with stairs on it came to the side of the plane and docked. When the plane door opened, a gush of hot air filled the entire plane. Aggrey, Phumla, Sandile and Nobuhlali were quick to take off their warm winter jackets from Sweden. The pilot announced that the weather was at 43 Celsius and that the passengers should prepare for a warm, sunny day with rain expected in the afternoon.

As they made their way off the plane, Sandile was reminded of the many Swedish sauna parties that he had attended. The air was moist and his eyes were tearing up from the heat mixed with a bit of humidity. His father Aggrey was walking down the plane stairs with him.

"Tata, is it always this hot here?"

"Most of the time, son, with some reprieves during the rainy season, but generally it's always hot."

There was some confusion when they got to the passport counter at arrivals. Aggrey was the only member of his family with a Ghanaian passport whilst the rest carried South African passports with an unstamped American visa. Aggrey quickly explained to the lady behind the passport counter their history and how they had left South Africa, without leaving out any detail. The lady behind the counter, although she had heard numerous stories of this sort from travellers, seemed to be engrossed in the story.

When Aggrey stopped speaking, she sat there staring at him, expecting more. He could see she was enjoying herself, so he decided to amuse her and carry on. He told her how the children had never seen their grandfather and he was almost at the end of his days and he wanted them to meet him before he passed on. He concluded by repeating what she had heard on so many occasions: that we lived in difficult times. When he said that, she concurred and begun stamping each one of their passports, one by one. She bundled them up and gave them to Aggrey when she was finished and wished him a happy return home with his family.

All of the conversation had been in Fanti but somehow Phumla, Sandile and Nobuhlali seemed to follow the gist of the conversation. As they walked out of the airport, Aggrey asked them if he should explain to them what he was speaking about with the lady behind the passport counter and they all said no, they had understood everything just fine. Aggrey thought to himself this was the magic of the continent. Africa could have more than a thousand dialects and people still understood one another across border and nationality. He exclaimed to himself, "Uhuru!"

The children overheard him and also exclaimed in unison, "Uhuru, Tata!"

He had a greater sense of comfort that his family members would be able to understand his broken English mixed with a bit of Fanti here and there.

Although his father Jonas had not been able to pick them up from the airport, he had organised a small minibus to bring them to his house in East Lagon. Aggrey had been sending money back home to his father for a number of years now, to assist him to build a house in a new residential area in Accra, not so far from the airport. His father had been living in the house, which was rather big for one person, for two years. According to his letters, he often felt lonely and yearned from the company of other people. Aggrey's cousin Kwesi lived with and took care of his father, but they seldom spoke as Kwesi was in his early thirties and they did not have that much in common. Jonas' wife Agnus, Aggrey's mother, had died from birth complications, shortly after delivering Aggrey in 1954.

Aggrey had not been back to Ghana since he had left in the early seventies. During that times, most Ghanaian academics had fled to other African nations and America because they feared reprisals from the military government. It was what Jonas referred to as the dark years of Ghanaian history. By 1990, with the release of Nelson Mandela, things were different. A lot of academics were coming back to

Ghana and Africa in general under a new wave of African optimism. Aggrey's family was one of those families that was returning from the diaspora.

Aggrey's father was overjoyed to see them and even lamented that the children looked like his late wife. He now walked with a cane, which was an affront to his confidence. Every now and then he would walk without his cane around the house to show his son he still had some youthful vigour. He wanted to put Aggrey's mind at ease that he did not have any feelings of abandonment by him and that he had coped fine over the years and could take care of himself.

He was proud of his son, who had a beautiful wife and two loving children. Over the week that they were in Accra, he spent many nights with the children, telling them stories of Ghanaian liberation and how Ghana was the first African nation to be liberated from colonialism. The children had many questions for him, and they wanted to know about the first president of Ghana, Kwame Nkrumah, who had become a mythical figure to them. To their dismay, Jonas was rather negative about Kwame Nkrumah, referring to him as the father of the "Africa must unite movement" but a coward.

He told them of the arrests during Kwame Nkrumah's time of other African liberation leaders such as J.B. Danquah, who died in prison in a liberated Ghana. According to Jonas, Nana Joseph Kwame Kyeretwie Boakye Danquah was born on the 18th of December 1895 and died on the 4th of February 1965. He was a Ghanaian statesman, pan Africanist, scholar, lawyer and historian. He played a significant role in pre- and post-colonial Ghana, which was formerly the Gold Coast, and in fact is credited with giving Ghana its name.

During his political career, Danquah was one of the primary opposition leaders to Ghanaian president and independence leader Kwame Nkrumah. J.B. Danquah was described as the "doyen of Gold Coast politics". He told them that Danquah was one of the most important leaders of a liberated Ghana whose contribution had been forgotten by history. He told them Danquah's death for him was the death of Uhuru in Ghana and that, since his death, the nation had taken a downward spiral after Nkrumah's atrocities.

In the same breath, he told them how visionary Kwame Nkrumah was for Ghana, even starting a Ghanaian nuclear and space program which never met its potential. According to Jonas, Nkrumah was so ahead of his time that he attracted the all-seeing eye of the US government, which had, in the end, had him killed.

The children were slowly learning some of the paradoxes of post-colonial Africa from their grandfather Jonas and they could not get enough. However, after he told them what the US government had done to Mr. Nkrumah, they understood why their parents had opted to live in Sweden rather than the United States of America. Jonas even went as far as to tell them that in their country of South Africa, an American agent was responsible for the imprisonment of Nelson Mandela because he had given away his location while he was an underground operative. This resulted in Nelson Mandela being sentenced to life imprisonment. He'd spent twenty-seven years in prison after the infamous South African treason trials.

The children could not bring themselves to tell their grandfather that their parents had accepted jobs in Kenya with the World Bank and IMF, which were American agencies. They had hoped that their parents would tell their grandfather but instead it became a family secret that their grandfather would go to his grave not knowing. Aggrey had told the children that his father was old and he did not feel like stressing him in his old age. The children became their parents' accomplices and kept their secret from Jonas.

Each night, instead of watching TV, they would sit at their grandfather's feet in the TV room and allow him to narrate story after story of the Africa he had known and loved. They also began to love Africa again through the eyes of their grandfather. They showered their grandfather with love and affection and for the week that they were there he felt as if he had known them all their lives.

On the last day of their week-long visit, Sandile and Nobuhlali woke up to their mother and father crying in the TV room. There was an ambulance outside with some people from the hospital walking in and out of their grandfather's room. Aggrey and Phumla informed the children that the time for their grandfather on this earth had come to an end. He had waited all these years to see his grandchildren and, now that he had, he was ready to go to the next place.

The children were shell shocked since it was the first time that they had visited their grandfather and they had grown to love him so much within a period of a week.

Aggrey was glad that Sandile in particular had met Jonas because it would give him a chance to further define what he understood to be manhood from the experience.

Although Jonas was a strict military man, the time he'd spent with his grandchildren was full of love and joy. For once, Aggrey had seen his father opening up in a way that he had never experienced before. He had showed the children unrestrained love in their time with him. He had hoped some of his father's spirit would rub off on Sandile and he would become less serious about his ideas of manhood and be able to live a meaningful life.

On many occasions, Aggrey had considered the rights of passage of young Xhosa men going to the mountains rather draconian and wished that they would modernise the practice. It was through his father that he hoped that Sandile's ideas of manhood were modernised and refined in his heart.

Phumla, his wife, took the death of Jonas very hard because it made her realise how little time her mother had left on this earth, and their return to South Africa in order to see her, was still some years away. She shed tears of loss for Jonas and also of longing for her mother. She was mourning two people and Aggrey had difficulty consoling her.

The only thing that made her stop crying was the children. Out of nowhere, not knowing how else to comfort their mother, the children said the Lord's Prayer together. By the time they were finished, Phumla had shed her last tear. Again, the children had found another reason to exclaim Uhuru and they did in unison. "Uhuru, Mama, Granddad is now free!" She was happy that the children had spiritual grounding from her mother Rhundu that would help them in difficult moments in life.

The family stayed another week in Ghana to organise Jonas' estate and to bury him in an Anglican funeral as per his last wishes. Their arrival in Nairobi after the death of Jonas would be a sombre affair. The trauma of Jonas' death would stay with the family for months to come. They had faced challenges together before, but the death of Jonas made them more worried about Rhundu and how long she had on earth. Their time in Kenya would be a learning and growth experience for the family, but with Rhundu's well-being always on top of mind for all of them.

The family spent another five years in Kenya, with the children attending a private school called Braeburn High School. The school was for children of government officials and ambassadors and had an international flavour to it. Although they met a lot of other young children, Sandile, Nobuhlali and Simon kept to themselves. They had gone through so much together and did not feel like bringing new people into their circle of trust to share their burdens. With each year that they spent in Kenya, the children drew closer and developed a support system amongst one another that would guide them through life. The children continued to learn about African culture and history in Kenya, especially African spiritual culture.

Simon's mother had a difficult time whilst living in Kenya. She missed her husband and desperately wished her family could be together and that the war in Sudan would come to an end so that she could move home. She was sick of her and Simon always fearing for their safety everywhere they went. She had lost her sense of privacy since their bodyguards went everywhere they went and were always shadowing her and her son.

Although Aggrey and Phumla tried to support her and show her she was loved, it was not enough. She could not cope with the loneliness and the spiritual toll on her and her son of war. She needed to find other ways to cope with her spirituality. She decided to get a job at a Kenyan NGO, working with people in rural areas to pass the time and keep her mind occupied. She fell in love with the culture of rural Kenya and also how people lived. On one of her many trips in the rural areas outside of Nairobi she came across an African shaman who told her that the war in Sudan would end soon and that she would be reunited with her husband. He also told her things about herself that she had never told anyone, and she fell into his magical grip.

Every day, when Simon had gone to school, she would start her days with the shaman for a consultation. Sometimes, the consultations would go on the whole day and she would get back home late. One day, she did not come back at the usual time and Simon asked Sandile and Nobuhlali to accompany him to the shaman's house. His mother had taken him there on a number of consultations to tell him about his future.

Sandile and Nobuhlali were now at an age where their parents let them go out on their own without having to ask for permission, since they were young adults. Nairobi was a safe city with minimal crime and the children were free to roam the city with their friend Simon. When they got to the shaman's house, they were met by an old lady who told them that Faeema, Simon's mother, was still in her consultation.

While they waited, the old lady took an interest in Sandile. She began walking around him several times and making gestures with her hands. Sandile was not sure whether to be afraid or to tell the old lady to go away. There was something that attracted Sandile to her, and he, like Simon and Nobuhlali, was interested in what she was doing. She began to speak in tongues and continue to circle around Sandile. Sandile was confused and decided to speak back to her.

"Mam, I don't understand what you are saying. Please speak English so I can understand."

She stopped circling around Sandile and looked at him in the eyes and began shaking. "I see them! I see them all around you."

Simon was annoyed with the woman, as that is how they'd drawn his mother in with their magic. He began shouting at the woman. "Get my mother now and stop this voodoo of yours, old lady."

The old woman looked down and could not face Simon. She was afraid of him, but she wanted to finish telling Sandile what she had started. She looked up at Sandile again and he could feel her penetrating energy.

"Young man, you don't see it now, but you are one of us. I can see the elders and ancestors all around you."

Nobuhlali was afraid for her brother and grabbed his hand. "Sandile, let's leave here. I don't feel right being in this place."

Sandile was curious but he did not have the energy to ask the old lady any questions and concurred with his sister. "Simon, Nobuhlali is right. Please get your mother and let's go from here."

The old woman began walking back from Sandile whilst addressing him as if she was avoiding something. "There are so many of them. Young man, if you do not learn to speak to them, they will drive you to madness! Mark my words: acknowledge them and you will be at peace with them and yourself."

Sandile was about to respond to the old lady but Simon's mother came out of the house with the shaman. "Oh, children! You did not have to come all this way for me. I was on my way home. In fact, this will be the last time I will be coming here as the shaman is done with me now. However, he says one of you children needs a consultation to speak to your ancestors."

The shaman pointed at Sandile but Nobuhlali was pulling him away from the old woman and the shaman.

"Sandile, we have to go. We don't understand this magic. We must go now before we are lost. I know you have questions, but we must leave here before we are drawn into something we don't understand."

The shaman looked at Sandile and then his sister Nobuhlali and said, "Uhuru, my children, Uhuru. Leave in peace."

Faeema, Simon, Sandile and Nobuhlali left the shaman's house after his comments and never returned.

The shaman and the old woman would stay in Sandile's thoughts for months to come, but he would never discuss it with his sister or Simon. He thought about what they could have meant and what they saw in him, and he could not for the life of him figure it out.

The shaman had cured Simon's mother of her loneliness and she never went back to see him again. She continued her work with people in the rural areas for her NGO and she was a picture of happiness. Aggrey and Phumla would often remark to their children that the magic of the shaman was nothing short of a miracle for Faeema. She had a new sense of meaning and she was generally upbeat and happy all of the time. She was a new person.

Sandile's father referred to the shaman's magic as undocumented African indigenous capital. He told Sandile and Nobuhlali that there were many mysteries on the African continent that had been buried by the savagery of colonialism and apartheid.

Sandile went as far as to ask his father if he thought African magic existed. His father concurred that he had seen African shaman perform miracles when he was a child in Ghana, but he did not know how they did it. Some of them performed miracles through herbs and some of them through divination with the ancestors. It was all a mystery to Aggrey, but he told Sandile he believed in African magic.

Phumla also concurred that on many occasions in her social work in South Africa and Zimbabwe she had seen shaman healing people, especially those who suffered from trauma. They did this through herbs and divination with the ancestors. However, to Phumla the old ways of spiritual Africa were lost and some of the African shaman were giving people empty promises and not healing them.

Phumla told Sandile how her mother Rhundu came from a long line of healers and that at one stage in her life she had practised as an inyanga or traditional herbalist, before she became religious.

There were so many unanswered questions on African spirituality for Sandile and Nobuhlali in Kenya but the visit to the shaman's house had piqued their interest. It was an aspect of African culture that they had yet to discover. They had become curious about African magic and they wanted to learn more.

Sandile often thought to himself that the ancestors had not forgiven him for not going to the mountains after his circumcision and at some point in the future they were going to drive him mad, as per the old lady's statement. Perhaps it would be the pregnancy of Anelisa in his dream that would finally drive him mad by shattering some of the expectations he had grown up having about him and her.

Over the years he had missed her terribly and his love for her had grown. He had met many young women who had taken an interest in him, but he had always deterred them from forming a relationship with him. He was saving himself for Anelisa because he had promised his manhood to her all those years ago. He knew that his father considered going to the mountains a bit draconian and outdated, so he did not bring the issue up with him. He would often ask his father leading questions about African spiritual beliefs and how they worked, but nothing specific enough as to make the questions point back to an experience he was now having.

Since the visit to the African Shaman's house in the rural areas of Nairobi, he began to have a lot of intense dreams about his grandfather Jonas. In his dreams, he would often tell him to do a ceremony to pacify the ancestors for not having gone to the mountains. In the dream, he told Sandile that he had to slaughter a sheep and pray with his family for their blessing. His grandfather told him in his dreams that he knew that Sandile had lived through some difficult times during apartheid and the ancestors were willing to forgive him, but he had to commune with them in order to receive their blessings for not going to the mountains.

His grandfather concluded the dreams by saying that, if he did not commune with the ancestors for guidance and for their blessing, then they would make his life difficult and he would have a difficult manhood throughout his life. He would lose Anelisa to another older man and she would become pregnant by him.

The same dream would repeat itself over and over and it was driving Sandile to the brink of madness. He did not know how to tell his father about it.

One day, when he was having a spirited conversation with his father, he finally got the courage to narrate his dream to him. His father listened intently to Sandile and then gave him a very simple answer, one which he did not expect. He told him that Sandile's grandfather had also had intense visions when he was younger. He tried everything to make the visions go away, but they got worse each day. It was shortly before his wife Agnus passed away. The visions were driving Jonas to the brink of madness and he had difficultly deciphering what was real and what was not. The visions would come in his sleep and when he was awake.

He then decided to consult a local shaman in a nearby village in Accra. After consulting the shaman, Jonas discovered that when he married Agnus he had never acknowledged his ancestors in a traditional wedding with Agnus and had only had a white ceremony. The ancestors wanted to be acknowledged before Agnus passed away so that she would rest easy in the next life.

Jonas then slaughtered a sheep and invited all his family members and his priest, and they prayed for the ancestor's forgiveness. Soon after that prayer, his visions went away, and his wife Agnus died peacefully.

Aggrey then started talking about Sandile's circumcision. He told him there was still one final step to his circumcision that they had to go through and that would be appealing to the ancestors for their blessing on his manhood. He had often thought of having a ceremony in Sweden to appease the ancestors for Sandile, but he told him that it would not have been a cultural norm in Sweden to slaughter a sheep at one's home, and people might have thought it quite peculiar and could have reported them to the authorities.

He told Sandile that he wanted to wait until they arrived in South Africa in the village of Cofimvaba in order to consult the elder of the family, his grandmother, who would be able to guide the ceremony for him.

Sandile asked him if the fact that Rhundu was a woman might cause any complications for him in the spiritual realm, with her leading the ceremony. Jonas told him that in his mind he did not consider that the ancestors took strong gender positions when people appealed to them for their blessings. What was most important was that people appealed to them, nevertheless.

He went further and told him that, when he'd first met Rhundu shortly after meeting his mother Phumla, in the early seventies, Rhundu was a practising inyanga or a traditional doctor, dealing with traditional herbs as a form of healing. This was before she became religious. He told Sandile that she would have the knowledge of appealing to the ancestors for him to be guided through his manhood through a blessing from the ancestors. He concluded by telling Sandile that, if he did not ask the ancestors for their blessings, he might be driven to the brink of madness like Jonas was, and that his life might be more difficult than it needed to be.

From that day on, Sandile knew he had one more step before his manhood was concluded and he could be with Anelisa. He feared the ancestors because of his dreams, but he knew in his heart it was a final step that he had to take in order to be fully a man. It would be his Uhuru moment, that being freedom from the constraints of childhood.

After three years of living in Kenya, his parent's contracts with the World Bank and IMF had come to an end. The year was 1994 and South Africa had had its first democratic election. They felt that it was now safe to go back home because the government had changed hands. They were also desperate to see Rhundu and missed her dearly. They felt that they were not complete as a family without her presence.

The children were now young adults. They had both finished high school and their parents thought it would be best for them to go to university in South Africa, the country of their birth.

Simon decided to pursue his studies in Kenya at the University of Nairobi and would stay behind, although it would not be the last time they would see him.

Simon and his mother wanted to be closer to Mr. John Garang by living in Kenya. Aggrey and Phumla's family was finally making their last move home after having lived in two countries. They were glad that they could finally return home, with so many wonderful memories of Sweden and Kenya to hold on to.

7

When Sandile's family arrived in Johannesburg airport from Nairobi, they could feel the wave of Afro optimism in the air. It was so intense that it was almost tangible. Nelson Mandela had been sworn in as president a couple of days prior to their arrival. Aggrey and Phumla, after their stints with the World Bank and the IMF, had decided that they did not want to work for large multinational institutions again and would start their own consulting business.

They had saved up a fair amount of money in their years of employment by the World Bank and IMF, and had managed to save in US dollars. They were also not completely convinced, after their tenure with the institutions, that American firms were sincere about real change on the African continent. They had witnessed negative development approaches to the continent by the institutions they served. This confirmed to them that they were nothing less than neo-colonial attempts to indirectly colonise the African continent through unfair lending and trading practices.

By the time that they'd arrived in Kenya in 1990, America had bought into the Washington Consensus. The Washington Consensus is a set of ten economic policy recommendations that were recommended to developing nations by Washington, D.C.–based institutions such as the International Monetary Fund (IMF), World Bank, and the US Treasury Department. It was coined in 1989 by English economist John Williamson.

The recommendations were really about how to open up African markets to a globalised world by making Africa and other developing nations more liberal in their trading and development policies. Aggrey and Phumla, in their tenure at the IMF and World Bank, always had a quote by the man who coined the Washington Consensus in the front of their minds whilst they worked there.

John Williamson went on to discuss the disasters brought about by the West's neoliberal policies by saying the following: *It is difficult even for the creator of the term to deny that the phrase "Washington Consensus" is a damaged brand name. Audiences the world over seem to believe that this signifies a set of neoliberal policies that have been imposed on hapless countries by the Washington-based international financial institutions and have led them to crisis and misery. There are people who cannot utter the term without foaming at the mouth.*

According to Aggrey and Phumla, they did not renew their contracts because the Washington Consensus had negative effects on development for African states. They told the children that the neoliberal policies of the West culminated in debt-strapped African nations. The African nations receiving the debt from the US focused mostly on export-led growth as a result of these policies. This export-led growth led to African states not being able to design their own secondary and tertiary industries for local production. They relied mostly on exporting their raw materials to other countries, where they would be turned into finished goods in the West and the sold back to African states at a premium.

Also, a lot of these African states were not able to protect their own local industries in a post-colonial era because of trade liberalisation, which also resulted in the wide-scale selling of African national assets for very low prices in order to maintain the debt positions to the IMF and World Bank.

Aggrey and Phumla felt that they were doing more harm than good by working at the IMF and World Bank. They thought they could contribute more to the African continent by setting up their own consulting company. This company would continue to work on the NEPAD document they had committed to all those years ago under Prime Minister Olof Palme, along with other African academics.

The consulting company would consult to African states on public policy and also provide scenarios of the future for them. Aggrey and Phumla developed a fascination with the discussions around ubuntu-led transformation and institutional reform in South Africa and thought they could be part of the national debate through their consulting firm. Aggrey and Phumla's understanding of ubuntu was that "ubuntu" was political philosophy that had aspects of socialism, propagating the redistribution of wealth. This was similar to redistributive policies in liberalism. However, at the same time it also had deeper societal connotations in that people often understood it as "a person is a person through other people and when I dehumanise you, I dehumanise myself".

They wanted to use Ubuntu philosophy as a basis for the values that would drive their consulting company, but over time the term ubuntu would take on more connotations in their lives with the rediscovery of their culture and their collective spirituality as a family. Through one another they would discover their destiny as a family and renew bonds to their continent of Africa through the spirit if ubuntu.

Aggrey and Phumla moved their family to Johannesburg and a suburb called Hydepark. It was in between the old city of Johannesburg but closer to the new centre of Johannesburg called Sandton. Although they had not seen Rhundu in a long time, they had to settle into life in Johannesburg and delayed going to Cofimvaba to see her until an appropriate time arose. However, for the first time in years they could contact her directly and speak to her without any subterfuge or fear of the security police.

Sandile also used the opportunity of coming back home to get in touch with Anelisa. She had grown to be a mature young woman, but Sandile could tell she still had her caring nature and that she still cared deeply for him.

One of the first things he wanted to find out when he started speaking to her was if she was pregnant or had had a child by another man. He could not ask her directly, out of fear of offending her, but he would often ask leading questions during their conversations. It did not take Anelisa long to figure out that he wanted to know if she had waited for him throughout the years as well. To his satisfaction, she appeased his ego and told him she had always remembered the promise that he'd made to her as children that he would come back for her as man and thus she'd waited for his return.

She had enrolled at the University of the Western Cape and she was studying law. Ever since she was young, she'd had a passion for justice and so she'd decided to pursue a field of practice that best represented her personality.

Nobuhlali had also kept in touch with Simon, both by phone and through letters. Sandile on many occasions tried to gain some information from her on how her relationship with Simon had progressed, but she was like a locked vault. She seldom gave him any information about what they spoke about, or any indication of the progression of their relationship. Sandile did not keep in close contact with Simon and relied on what little information his sister gave him to find out about his well-being.

Sandile and Nobuhlali also had to settle into the routine of attending university lectures and life in general in Johannesburg. They both enrolled at the University of the Witwatersrand in central old Johannesburg. Sandile was studying psychology, since he had always been preoccupied with human behaviour and how people made decisions and, to a certain degree, the culture of human behaviour.

Nobuhlali decided to follow her mother's footsteps by studying sociology with the intention of becoming a social worker when she finished studying.

Aggrey and Phumla insisted that the children study the social sciences because they thought it would better prepare them to improve the world that they lived in. According to them, South Africa was a country with numerous challenges that could best be assessed and understood through the study of social sciences. They could always study financial courses as their electives if they also wanted to understand the commercial world, but social sciences for Aggrey and Phumla were a must for them.

Socially, Sandile and Nobuhlali settled into the new South Africa and they managed to make new friends. Slowly, they begun to let their guard down in South Africa and they started feeling safe again in their own country. They had grown up in a different South Africa to the one that they lived in now. The South Africa they had known was politically volatile and unkind to black people.

There were still a lot of social issues that South Africans needed to contend with, especially the divide between the rich and the poor. However, the optimism in the people, both young and old, was contagious and Sandile and Nobuhlali also inherited that feeling. They lived in a new South Africa where anything was possible, and everyone was bandying the term ubuntu about.

Everywhere you went, people were talking about ubuntu and the new South Africa. Not a day went by when the word ubuntu was not mentioned somewhere. Racial barriers were falling down, and people did not have the patience for any people with a racist orientation. Within one election, the old South Africa had become illegal. This unleashed the potential of a unified nation.

Nelson Mandela's forgiving nature had become the national example of the spirit of ubuntu and he had created a national buy in into this spirit through the Truth and Reconciliation Commission headed up by Bishop Tutu. The atrocities of the past were being spoken about openly and people were forgiving one another for historical political crimes. There were, however, those like the apartheid agent Eugene De Kock, who'd committed crimes so heinous that they were sent to prison, even after they'd testified at the commission.

Former politicians under the apartheid government denied that they knew of these renegade actions and said that people like De Kock did not act on behalf of the state. They claimed that he had acted as a rogue agent.

The country was no longer on a knife-edge as it had been when Sandile and Nobuhlali's family had fled it in 1985 during the state of emergency. The nation was slowly beginning to heal its wounds and beginning to form a new social fabric that was inclusive of all of its races and cultures. The spirit of ubuntu was in the air.

A year passed after their arrival in South Africa before the family could go to Cofimvaba to visit Rhundu. Sandile continued to have his intense dreams with his grandfather narrating the same issue over and over. He had to go and ask for the ancestors' blessings or he would lose Anelisa to another man and he would have a difficult time through life.

Aside from his dreams, his general health started taking a turn for the worse. His sister Nobuhlali alerted his parents Aggrey and Phumla to the fact that Sandile's moods were becoming rather extreme. He no longer had the patience that he used to have and would often snap at his sister for the slightest infractions. On some days, he was really happy and on some really sad.

His parents just thought it was the pressures of having to adjust to three different cultures on his many moves around the world. They thought cultural integration was taking a toll on him more than his sister, who seemed to have settled well in South Africa. On numerous occasions his parents tried to gauge if there was something else bothering him, apart from adjusting to the new South Africa, and he told them about his repetitive dream and his grandfather Jonas speaking to him.

He told them how the dreams had become more intense and that he was now having them in the day time and he could clearly hear his grandfather Jonas' voice, even when he was awake. His grandfather's message was gnawing away at his grasp of reality and he could not cope with little things like having light-hearted conversations with people. One moment he would be really happy and then another moment really sad. He could no longer control his emotions.

His mother Phumla had seen these symptoms before in her work in Zimbabwe, with young adults who had suffered the horrors of war developing mental illness, particularly bipolar disorder and schizophrenia. These were severe mental illnesses but manageable with the right medication and treatment. She thought perhaps Sandile had not let go of the past and in some way he had been traumatised by the events of his youth during apartheid. This trauma was now surfacing as a mental illness, for which he needed treatment.

Sandile's father, on the other hand, took a more spiritual angle and blamed himself for not performing a spiritual ceremony with Sandile and the family to appease the ancestors for Sandile not going to the mountains after his circumcision. He had seen how the ancestors had affected his father and they were now affecting his son. After his father had performed the ceremony to appease the ancestors his visions had gone away. He was hoping he could do the same for Sandile by approaching the ancestors for their blessing of his manhood.

However, at first, before recommending the spiritual recourse for Sandile's affliction, Aggrey listened to his wife Phumla's perspective and agreed that their son should see a psychiatrist. They found a psychiatry clinic in the neighbouring suburb Randburg. It was called Crescent Clinic. There Sandile met a young white female doctor named Petra. Petra spoke to Sandile for about forty-five minutes. She asked him about his past and if he could remember any traumatic experiences that he'd had.

He told her about when he'd had to leave South Africa because the security police were after his father. He told her how stressed he was that he'd had to leave Anelisa behind. He told her how difficult it was for him to trust Mr. Dabula when he'd told him he had to leave the country on the day he'd left. He then also told her about travelling to East London airport with Mr. Andreas. He'd felt abandoned by Mr. Andreas when he left him at the airport all on his own and told him he would have to travel to London on his own.

He spoke about how difficult it was to leave his grandmother behind and that he had worried about her and her well-being every day when he was overseas. He spoke about the emotional toll, worrying that one day the security police would catch up to their family, wherever they were in the world, and being on guard all the time. He told her how, even in Sweden, they were on guard, especially after the assassination of the prime minister of Sweden Mr. Olof Palme.

He told her about wanting to be a man so that one day he could protect his family as he did and that it was one of the greatest aspirations of his life. As he told his story she managed to follow until he begun talking about his visions. To African people, visions from the ancestors were common but, when he begun narrating his visions, his doctor Petra had a perplexed look on her face. He could not tell if it was an expression of disappointment or interest, but he continued with his story.

He told her how, over the years, he had the same vision from his dead grandfather Jonas and that he wanted him to perform a ceremony to receive the blessings of the ancestor. He told her that the visions were starting to happen during the day, and he was not sure any longer of what was reality and what was not.

Immediately after he finished telling her about his visions, she told him she was sure that he had bipolar disorder and recommended that he allow himself to be admitted for a week or two. She had not understood Sandile's vision, and she found the story rather foreign, and he could pick up on it. However, at the same time he wanted something to help him with his extreme moods, so he agreed to being admitted to the clinic for observation and treatment for the condition of bipolar that he had been given.

His parents took the admission with great difficulty and they blamed themselves for Sandile's predicament. If only they had not been politically active during apartheid, then their son would be fine. Sandile's father was rather apprehensive about the treatment. He wanted to support his wife but at the same time he knew he had to appease the ancestors. They both agreed that they should try the modern option first with Sandile's condition and, if he did not get better, then they would try the African way by approaching the ancestors for their blessing.

During his hospital stay, Sandile came across Linda, who had also been admitted to the hospital. Every night, Linda would go to bed screaming, "Leaders, leaders, leaders!" During the course of the nights, he would scream the same words over and over again in his sleep. Sandile could not bring himself to ask Linda what he was on about. When he spoke to Linda during the day, he seemed very sound, and he could express himself very well. Every now and then Linda would say something definitive, like that the sun was following him, with no explanation for how he had arrived at this conclusion.

Linda told Sandile how he had wound up at the hospital. He told Sandile how he had got into a physical fight with his cousin and that his cousin had struck him on the head. Ever since that fight, Linda had been having these intense dreams about his ancestors that he could not manage and that is how he landed in the hospital. They both concurred that they should not have told Dr. Petra about their visions and should have kept their explanations to her brief and succinct.

Sandile knew that the only way he was going to be discharged from the hospital would be by telling his doctor that he was no longer having the visions and that the medication he was being given had made them go away.

On numerous occasions, Anelisa wanted to come and see Sandile in the hospital and he refused. He had not seen her since he'd come back to South Africa and he did not want her to see him in this helpless condition. His manhood simply would not be able to cope. Since she could not see him, she wrote him a letter in which she expressed her concern about his condition. However, at the same time she expressed more clearly than she ever had, eloquently, how much she loved and missed him. She wanted to be part of his life again in person and told him how difficult the years had been without his presence.

Upon receiving this letter, Sandile made a commitment that he would try to get better for Anelisa. In the clinic, he began reading as much as he could about bipolar. He found out that it was a mood disorder where one's mood would rapidly fluctuate between happy and sad. He found out that there were two kinds of bipolar and he had bipolar two, where he was constantly depressed or sad, with some moments of extreme happiness. He knew he could not be the kind of man that Anelisa deserved without learning to manage this condition and therefore also studied a bit about the medication that he was receiving for his condition, in order to cope with the side effects of drowsiness and poor attention that he was experiencing from it.

His doctor assured him that side effects were temporary and that after a while they would reduce. He landed up spending three weeks in the clinic. Although the pills he was taking balanced out his moods and he no longer had extreme mood swings, the visions from his grandfather still haunted him. He knew that if he told his doctor Petra about the visions, she would keep him in the clinic longer, so he kept them to himself and Linda.

After three weeks, Petra surmised that he was stable enough to go home but said that he should continue taking his pills. Although the pills worked to manage his mood swings, they also took away some of his humanity. He found he had difficulty being happy or sad: he was just in a zombie-like state.

It was then that he decided that he had to pursue other options to getting better that were more traditional. There was no way he could be with Anelisa in his current state with the effect the pills were having on him. His libido was also negatively affected, and he thought that the pills had taken away his manhood as well as his feelings.

When he spoke to his father Aggrey about the effects of the pills, he immediately contacted Rhundu and begun making plans for Sandile to undergo a ceremony in Cofimvaba to appease the ancestors. Perhaps in doing so it would also assist him with his bipolar and the negative effects of the pills he was taking. Sandile's mother did not consider it to be the best option but at that stage of Sandile's condition and the effects of the pills it was the only option.

It had been a year since Sandile's family had arrived in South Africa when he was released from the clinic. Rhundu was overjoyed that her family was finally returning home to the village of Cofimvaba. She had wished it had been under different circumstances, but who could predict the will of God? She made plans with the village elders to put together the ceremony for Sandile. She contacted the elders of the village church, which she had helped to build, to use the church grounds for the ceremony.

Although retired, Mr. Dabula, Sandile's old principal, wanted to lead the prayer service at the ritual. He was also a certified priest. Rhundu agreed because he had always been an honest and upright man and she thought the ancestors would be open to his prayers. Rhundu also invited Anelisa to the event, since she had been such a big part of Sandile's life. She did it in secret without informing Sandile and his family. She wanted to surprise him on his return to the village of his birth, and she wished for it to be full of love and deep African spirituality.

Rhundu had grown up in an age where ubuntu was defined as how people related to their community as being a greater extension of that community in their individuality. Sandile, who was now going through a difficult chapter in his life, had grown up as a member of that community; she considered it only right that she should involve the community within the ritual.

She wanted to be respectful of Aggrey's Fanti culture too, so she asked him if there was any aspect of the ceremony that he would like to lead. He told her that he had consulted the old African shaman who had helped his father when he'd fallen spiritually ill and he would like to make plans for the shaman to be present at the ceremony and to also say some words for Sandile. Rhundu concurred with him and she also told him of her plans to involve the local church and community elders, and Sandile's old principal in the event.

Aggrey was reminded of how efficient Rhundu was. He thought back to the eighties when he had called her one night, frantic that the security police were pursuing him. Rhundu had managed to calm him down and told him not to worry, as she would handle his plans to leave the country with the local community in Cofimvaba. Within twenty-four hour of his call to her she and the community had devised a plan for Nobuhlali to be whisked away from her Catholic school to meet him in Johannesburg to go to London. The following day, she'd made plans for Sandile to also leave the country to meet him in London.

Aggrey considered Rhundu to be a principled pragmatist and a very important person in the life of his family. He knew that she would be the perfect person to make the plans for the event for Sandile. She was thorough and very forward thinking. This is what had attracted members of the underground to her during the apartheid days. Although she had never joined any specific political party, she had been to military training in Zambia, Kenya and Tanzania. On each occasion, she was asked by some of the liberation parties in South Africa to make her own plans to get to her military training to assist underground operatives moving in and out of the then homelands of South Africa. She'd left and returned to the country on three separate occasions for military training during apartheid without ever getting caught.

During apartheid she was the one who planned the movements of operatives in her region of the country, which was the Transkei. The operatives she managed never got caught by the apartheid state, not even on the rare occasion when mistakes were made. She excelled at espionage and information gathering. The local village church she had helped to build was a hotbed of information gathering as people from surrounding villages would bring news of other operatives, who were hiding out in the rural areas.

The priests were usually the centre of the information gathering for the church since everyone in the church consulted the priest. Rhundu was the secretary of the church and she could spend long periods of time making plans with her church priest without the apartheid government suspecting foul play.

Through her spaza shop, she also took care of a lot of families who had lost their breadwinners due to the apartheid state. The apartheid state tried to recruit her as a double agent on numerous occasions, since they knew the work that her husband had been involved in and how influential she was in her community. Each time they made an inappropriate advance for her services, she always found unique ways to turn them down without incurring their ire or anger. She had a strong, unquestionable belief in God that had guided her through some difficult times and provided hope when none existed.

This was how the community came to know her as the woman of God of the village of Cofimvaba. Whenever a way could not be found to move operatives around the Transkei, she would simply ask them to trust in the knowledge that God would guide them. Over the years, she earned respect and reverence from her community for the work she did for South African liberation. For her community, she was the embodiment of ubuntu.

When the elders of the community were made aware of Sandile's condition, they were more than happy to help because of the work she had done in the community over the years.

A WEEK BEFORE the event and Sandile's family's arrival, the village elders called a meeting with Rhundu to discuss what had to be accomplished on the day of the event. She told them about Sandile's sudden onset of bipolar illness. His parents could not identify if it had been caused by stress early in his life or if it was because of a spiritual affliction caused by the fact that he had not appeased the ancestors by going to the mountains after his circumcision.

The elders narrated stories of young men in the village of Cofimvaba who were opting to go to the local clinic instead of going to the mountains because of all the deaths that were happening at initiation schools in the mountains. Young men were getting infections after their circumcision and some were not healing from their wounds adequately. Some of the mishaps were due to poorly trained surgeons, and some issues were just naturally happening. Whatever the case was, the elders in the village were sincerely rethinking the initiation of young men in the village. They were recommending to most of those who were preparing for their rights of passage that they get circumcised in the local clinic, followed by a traditional ceremony to appease the ancestors in their places of worship.

The elders of the village all agreed that traditional practices also had to be modernised and they did not want to be stuck in the past. Times had changed and going to the mountains for them was not the only way to ascend to manhood. This for them would not be the first time they would be doing a traditional ceremony of this nature and it had become commonplace within the village over the years.

They all knew Rhundu used to be a practising inyanga or a herbal healer before she became religious and asked her if Sandile's illness was perhaps not the onset of the spiritual illness ukthwasa. She told them that Sandile had been having a repetitive dream of speaking to his grandfather from Ghana about appeasing the ancestors and that the dream would not go away, even when he took the white man's medicine.

Sandile's father wanted a shaman from Ghana to be present at the traditional ceremony to pray for Sandile using Fanti tradition. The illness had all the signs of ukthwasa, but she would not be able to tell for sure until Sandile was in front of her. In Ghana it might not be known as ukthwasa and they might have different ways to handle the illness there.

The elders all concurred that, because Sandile was half Xhosa and half Ghanaian, it would be best for the shaman from Ghana to lead the proceedings. They, the elders, would be present to assist with the prayers and slaughtering of the sheep and for moral support. They further concurred that it would be in order for Mr. Dabula to lead the prayers in order to represent Sandile's Xhosa heritage in the ceremony. But, in the main, the Ghanaian shaman would lead the proceedings.

When Rhundu was done with the preparations and consultation with the village elders, she informed Aggrey that he could come to Cofimvaba the following weekend and that all the arrangements had been made.

The following weekend, Aggrey and his family got on a plane to Umtata, from where they would travel by car to Cofimvaba. When they landed, the first thing they all noticed were the rolling hills of the Transkei with a low misty fog over the mountains. Sandile felt as if he had done a full circle. He had left the intimacy of his village of Cofimvaba, seeking safety with his family in foreign lands. He was now back to the land of his birth to ask the ancestors to guide him in this chapter of his life and bless his manhood. The route he took to Cofimvaba from Umtata was the same route he had used with Mr. Andreas to flee the country.

He thought about the feeling of leaving something important behind. He had left behind his culture and tradition in the hopes of one day returning as a man to claim his cultural manifest destiny and the woman he loved, Anelisa. On the drive to Cofimvaba, every now and then Sandile would catch scents of cow dung mixed with grass which reminded him of his youth. He imagined himself as a child walking Anelisa to school, reciting the biblical stories his grandmother had told him the night before. He could see her patient and loving smile and he felt the comfort and confidence it gave him.

He thought about all the times she had protected his interests without being asked and her never-ending loyalty to him when they were children. He thought back to the days his teacher Mrs. Nontish would address him as inkwenkwe, and how he'd hated being called boy. He thought about how she never ran out of energy to discipline him and how she derived joy from, when she was finished, sending him to the principal's office.

All the memories of his youth came flooding back and he could feel them healing and nurturing his soul. The village of Cofimvaba and its people had a record of his life, which in his mind was the purest and most innocent chapter of his life. He desperately wanted to reclaim that innocence again in order to renew his hopes and his dreams for manhood. This trip home would be more than a ceremony to appease the ancestors and ask them for their blessing; it would also be his spiritual redemption.

When they arrived in Cofimvaba, the elders of the village and the shaman from Ghana were waiting for Sandile in his grandmother's driveway. The Ghanaian shaman was dressed in a beautiful and colourful kente cloth outfit, which set him apart from the village elders, who were all wearing dark suits. He tried to look around but he could not see Mr. Dabula. There were no women around and it was just a group of men. Sandile thought the woman were inside the house.

When the family got out of the car, Sandile saw his grandmother emerging from behind the group of men. Without saying a word, she kindly escorted his mother Phumla and his sister Nobuhlali in the direction of the village church. Mr. Mamphese, who was the most senior of the village elders, told Sandile and his father Aggrey that all the women in the family were in a church service with Mr. Dabula at the local church and that they would not go inside the church with the women.

Mr. Mamphese addressed Sandile as ikwedini, which was young man, but still not yet a man. Sandile had always respected Mr. Mamphese, as he and his grandmother Rhundu had been very close when he was a boy. He decided to follow his guidance on that day, as he had on so many occasions as a child. He looked down at Sandile and told him that there was a place for women and a place for men and he hoped that Sandile understood this. Sandile simply nodded his head in agreement.

Mr. Mamphese was a skinny, tall, fair skinned man with bi-focal glasses. He had on many occasions before used his height and baritone voice to command respect amongst his peers. Mr. Mamphese told them that they would go to the local church as well and would listen to Mr. Dabula's prayers from outside the church until he was finished, and then they would accompany the shaman to perform the duties he had come for.

The village elders had created a small kraal at back of the church where the shaman would perform his ceremony. The group of men and Sandile and his father stood outside the main door of the church and listened to Mr. Dabula's prayers for Sandile. Sandile could hear Mr. Dabula's sermon clearly over the loudspeakers. He spoke mostly about Sandile's ancestors and named each one of them, both from his mother's side and from his father's side. He then spoke about Sandile's childhood and what a great student he had been.

He then decided to tell the church about what he considered to be the greatest love story he had ever seen. He told the church about this young lady named Anelisa who had held on to the memory of a young man for over ten years. Anelisa had become increasingly religious over the years and relied on God to bless her love with Sandile and allow it to grow, even without his presence. He spoke about the undying loyalty of a young lady whose love inevitably would lead to the redemption of Sandile's soul.

According to Mr. Dabula, her love personified what he understood to be ubuntu in that Anelisa was a person through Sandile and him through her within their community. He described Anelisa's love for Sandile as a river flow, which traversed the most difficult mountain terrain from its source to get to the sea. Mr. Dabula concluded by saying that Anelisa was truly one of the meek children of God that are spoken about in the bible. Her perseverance in love surely would yield the ancestors' favour, both for her and Sandile in their future.

After his talk, Mr. Dabula said the Lord's prayer and the men slowly made their way from the main door of the church to the kraal at the back of the church. Sandile had tears in his eyes because he had never heard love described in the way that Mr. Dabula had described it. He also had a deeper appreciation for the sacrifice that Anelisa had made when he was not there. Throughout the years he had often thought about the sacrifice he had made in waiting for her, and how difficult things had been for him. He had never given enough attention to how difficult things might have been for her in the hostile environment of apartheid.

It was as if Anelisa had personally expressed her love for him through Mr. Dabula's words. He had tried to look for Anelisa amongst the women in the church, but he could not tell who was who from looking at the backs of the women.

He felt a bit of angst about the ceremony that was about to take place and he wished that he could have at least seen Anelisa from a distance, as that would have calmed his nerves a bit. But he knew there was no time more important than the present for him to be the man he had always dreamt about being one day.

He swallowed his apprehension and fear and proceeded with the other men to the back of the church and to the kraal. When they got to the kraal, there was a slaughtered sheep in the middle of the kraal. The body of the sheep had been separated from the skin and the body was resting on top of the skin. The shaman said the Lord's Prayer over the sheep, and then asked some of the older men in the village to carry the body of the sheep to where the women were preparing the food, so that they could cook the sheep. Aggrey assisted the elders in carrying the sheep. He asked them to leave the head of the sheep behind, resting on the sheepskin. They did as requested, and the shaman waited for them to return before proceeding with the ceremony.

There was a small steel basin near the sheep with a fire lit under it. The fire had been burning for some time in the kraal as Sandile could smell the burned wooden branches whose odour had surrounded the kraal. The shaman instructed all the men to sit in circle around the sheep head and the steel basin with the burning fire. Sandile was asked to sit in the centre of the circle, closest to the steel basin and the sheep's head. After they had all taken a seat, the shaman poked the eyes of the sheep's head out of their sockets and put them in the steel basin. The basin was so hot from the flames that it burned the eyes to black charcoal within seconds.

He told the group of men that the eyes of the sheep represented an offer to the ancestors in order to give Sandile new spiritual eyes. He then went to tell the group that in

Ghanaian culture the ancestors usually guided the living through difficulty in dream states. If the people did not listen to these dreams, then they could be driven to the brink of madness. But, in order to be able to comprehend the message from the ancestors, Sandile would have to see with new spiritual eyes.

Mr. Mamphese concurred with the shaman and told him that in South Africa there was a similar belief, that the soul had to be open to receiving guidance from the spiritual realm if one wanted to commune with the ancestors. He told him that offerings were largely ceremonial and differed from culture to culture or from tribe to tribe.

The shaman then asked Sandile to close his eyes and see with his new spiritual eyes and try to discern what his grandfather was trying to tell him, although he was not compelled to tell the rest of the group what he had experienced or would see with his new spiritual eyes. It would be for him and the woman he would one day make his wife to decipher the meaning of the message from his grandfather. According to the shaman, he would have to discern for himself what was at the core of his spiritual illness and only he could do this.

Sandile closed his eyes and immediately went into a deep trance. His father, the shaman and the elders of the village sat there observing Sandile closely. They tried to create a spiritually intimate environment for Sandile through absolute silence. They noticed that he had a glow that emanated from his person and the shaman whispered that this was the protective shield of the ancestors. The shaman told the group during Sandile's trance that he had seen this energy that surrounded Sandile on many other shamans whom he had encountered, and it usually meant the one bearing the energy had a calling from the ancestors to practise divination and help others.

The village elders confirmed their suspicions that they had discussed with Rhundu that Sandile was going through the spiritual illness of ukthwasa. The shaman stressed that Sandile had to take a personal journey within the spiritual realm if he were to get better and receive the blessing from the ancestors.

Whilst Sandile was in his trance, the shaman lit some incense and put it into the steel basin with the burned sheep eyes. He whispered that the scent of the burned incense would guide Sandile in his trance in the spiritual realm. Many of the village elders had seen people go into a spiritual trance before. The village elders in Cofimvaba, although not in this way, had performed many of these ceremonies of the rights of passage.

After half an hour of Sandile's trance, as if it were a natural act, they all held hands and started humming together and moving from side to side. The humming slowly became monotonous, and they were congruent with Sandile's energy. This only served to heighten Sandile's trance and they were now part of Sandile's spiritual initiation with the ancestors. They were sharing in the spirit of ubuntu. An hour passed by until Sandile came out of his trance. When he came out of his trance, the shaman told him he now had new spiritual eyes of the ancestors and he had traversed the spiritual realm in his trance.

The shaman asked Sandile to stand up and walk outside the kraal and the first woman he saw with his new spiritual eyes would be his wife. Sandile, although petrified, was also sensing a new energy within himself that quelled the fear in his soul. He slowly made his way out of the kraal and when he got to the entrance, he prayed the Lord's Prayer and repeated it over and over in his mind until he was ready.

When he opened his eyes, the most beautiful woman he had ever seen was standing in front of him and smiling. She had beautiful bronze skin. He felt like he was seeing Anelisa for the first time and the sight of her was breathtaking.

Sandile took a moment to take in Anelisa's beauty without saying a word. He stared at her for a while, looking her up and down. For the first time, he noticed her hourglass figure and her hips; they were inviting. When they were growing up, she did not have hips like that, and she had been a skinny and lanky girl. He thought about having intercourse with her. He imagined himself grasping her hips at the moment of ecstasy, and for a moment he was fulfilled.

He then moved his eyes up to her face. Her golden bronze skin was inviting, and he imagined himself giving her a kiss and how it would be. Would he kiss her with his mouth closed or would he kiss her with a mouth full of tongue? He had never had sex with a woman nor kissed one and these thoughts were nothing short of an immature emotional conjecture. Whatever the case, as per the shaman's predictions, she would be his wife as she was the first woman he set his eyes upon when he left the kraal. The only thing left now was to actually convince her of what the shaman said.

Another thought crossed his mind: maybe he should run to her and give her a hug. After all, he had not seen her in years. She stood there smiling at him, sending her overwhelming energy in his direction, waiting for him to take the lead. Perhaps she was a prisoner of this whole event. The community had an expectation of them and perhaps she was trapped in the euphoria of the moment. He wanted her to have the freedom of being with him, not because the community expected them to be together but because she wanted to. He wanted her to make a choice based on love rather than responsibility.

Perhaps she felt sorry for him and his condition and she was being kind and would let him down later, when they had spoken. He was no longer dreaming of his grandfather Jonas and the visions of warning. He was standing in front of the love of his life, and he was speechless.

Anelisa decided to be strong for both of them and broke the silence. "Sandile, this moment is happening. I hope you can come to grips with that!"

He knew that he would have to invite the woman whom he had seen with his spiritual eyes back into the kraal so that the shaman could bless her. He knew that the union had to be approved by the ancestors. However, he had so much to say and so much to explain. He wanted to tell her why it had taken a year since his arrival in South Africa for them to see one another again. He wanted to explain to her that the shaman had said that the first woman he saw with his spiritual eyes would be his wife, but he had no words.

He looked at her gentle hands and imagined himself walking with her into the kraal holding them. They would enter victorious. Time had not come in between their love; nor had the atrocities of apartheid. He stood there trying to make sense of her comments that this moment was happening, and that he should come to grips with it.

He decided to speak. He did not care what came out of his mouth as long as he responded to her comments. "Ntobi, I love you. I want to share my life with you. You represent my greatest potential, and I love you."

She was taken aback at his frankness. This was not the Sandile she knew, but a man who was settled in his love for her. He did not have to get on his knees and propose to her as white people did. She stared at the village child she once knew, who would spend hours looking for fresh cow dung in order to make her job easier. She thought about the boy who would memorise his grandmother's stories verbatim in order that she would also derive the same amount of joy as he did when he heard them for the first time. She thought about the boy who was emotionally immature and whose interests she had defended on so many occasions.

This young man was no longer that boy she'd once known. He was a man who had come to fulfil a promise to a woman who was once a tender young girl. He was a man of his word who had come to claim his destiny in her.

"Sandile, my friend and soul mate, I am prepared to follow if you will lead. I am prepared at this moment as I have been all of my youth and adult life to love you until death us do part."

Sandile reached out his hand to Anelisa and she came forward and placed her right hand in his left hand. She had remembered her mother's words that a woman should walk on a man's left side in order that the man might protect her from harm. She noticed that Sandile's hand was trembling, although he tried to make light of the situation by giving her an uncomfortable smile. He did not know what to say and thus he embraced her and tried to project every feeling of love and adoration for her through his hug. She took a deep breath and for the first time in years she knew that her heart was where it was meant to be. With her second breath she exclaimed out loud: "Ubuntu!"

8

Sandile and Anelisa walked into the kraal with the village elders, the shaman and Aggrey. They took a seat in the centre of the circle where Sandile had been sitting during his trance. The shaman took the incense from the steel bowl that was still alight and began making circular gestures around Sandile and Anelisa with it.

"May these children, this boy, now a man, and this girl, now a woman, see with the same spiritual eyes. May the two eyes offered up to the ancestors be a representation of both their new spiritual sight in life and in love. May the scent of this incense be a representation of the spirit that unites these two children in love and respect for one another.

"I call upon the ancestors to bless this union and for this ceremony to be a representation of these two children's spiritual union before their community. I call upon the spirit of Jonas, who has put this union together from the world beyond with his visions to Sandile, to now rest in the world beyond and to bless the union of these two children. I call upon the community elders and this father's child to lay hands on these two children in order to give them the community's blessings and a father's love and blessing."

Anelisa and Sandile both had their heads bowed down as a sign of respect for the shaman, the village elders and Aggrey. Aggrey stood up first and laid his hands on Sandile and Anelisa. The village elders followed suit. They all began humming again and moving from side to side. The shaman took the burned sheep eyes, which were now charcoal, and crushed them in his hands. He used the ash to draw crosses on Anelisa and Sandile's heads.

"We approach the Lord and His only begotten son Jesus Christ to bless the union that the ancestors have conceived. Amen."

The humming came to an end and the village elders and Aggrey took their seats in the circle. The shaman walked up to Aggrey and asked him if he blessed the union of the children.

"Yes, I bless the union of these two children with my heart and soul. My wife and I will guide them with the assistance of the ancestors and the Almighty God, in Whose presence we find ourselves, in this sacred space."

The shaman then walked over to Sandile and lifted his head so that he was looking directly at him.

"Young man, the ancestors have blessed you and your union, but you also have a choice to make. I can see from the spirit of the ancestors surrounding you that you are being called to be one of us. That is to be one who works with divination and communing with the ancestors. This has been the reason for your illness. You have a choice on this day. Either to continue your path to becoming one with the ancestors, where you can help others, which will bring much pain and heartache for you and the ones you love, or you can ask that they pick another to work through. If you say no, your sickness will leave you and you will live a peaceful life and the ancestors will bless all you do."

Sandile knew he did not want to be a shaman and had been through all he could handle with the ancestors. He was not ready to go through the rigorous process of being trained as a shaman. His father had told him when he was younger that some shaman trained for years before they were initiated, forsaking family and friends in the search for a spiritual life. He was not ready to make the sacrifice to share his new-found relationship with Anelisa with the ancestors and training to be a shaman.

"Sir, with all respect, I choose a life less lived and that is with my love Anelisa and my family. Although I am blessed to have been chosen by the ancestors, I would ask that they pick another to work through. I say this within the presence of my community and my father and may the ancestors make it so."

The shaman put his hands on Sandile's and Anelisa's foreheads.

"And so shall it be, young man. May the ancestors continue to bless all that you do. May they assist with the growth of your and your wife's souls in love, and bless your family both in this world and the next. In the presence of the ancestors and the mighty God, I bring this ceremony to its conclusion. If anyone has any objections to the events of this ceremony, kindly place your objections in front of the ancestors and the mighty Jehovah."

The shaman looked around the circle and everyone had their heads bowed down to the floor. The village elders started praying in unison.

"Our Father in heaven, hallowed be Your name. Your kingdom come, Your will be done, on earth as it is in heaven. Give us this day our daily bread, and forgive us our debts, as we also have forgiven our debtors. And lead us not into temptation but deliver us from evil. For Thine is the kingdom, the power and the glory, forever and ever. Amen"

The shaman put his hands in the air and exclaimed, "May it be according to the will of God!"

Before he said Amen he decided to conclude the ceremony by telling the elders of the village, Aggrey, Sandile and Anelisa the story of Amun Rah. According to the shaman, in his traditional beliefs Amun was the son of the Gods who carried prayers to the heavens and that was the reason that people said Amen after every prayer in order that they prayers would be carried to the heavens and the ancestors.

There was a silence and the shaman decided to continue with his history lesson. According to the shaman, Amun – also Amon, Ammon, Amen – was the ancient African Egyptian god of the sun and air. He was one of the most important gods of ancient Egypt and African traditional culture. He was usually depicted as a bearded man wearing a headdress with a double plume, or as a ram-headed man or simply a ram, symbolising fertility in his role as Amun-Rah.

His name means "the hidden one", "invisible", "mysterious of form" and, unlike most other Egyptian gods, he was considered Lord of All, who encompassed every aspect of creation.

Amun was associated with protecting the king but, largely, was an African fertility God. Amun was considered no more powerful or significant than the other gods. He represented the element of "hiddenness" or "obscurity", while the others represented more clearly defined concepts such as "darkness", "water" and "infinity". Amun as "the Obscure One" left room for people to define him according to their own understanding of what they needed him to be, and that was one who carried their prayers to the heavens. The shaman concluded: "Today, as in the days of old, we ask that Amun carry our prayers and ambitions to the netherworld of God and the ancestors so that Sandile's decision will be heard in the hereafter."

When the shaman had finished his little history lesson he said: "Amen". The elders of the village had a clear understanding after his lesson about the God Amun and why Aggrey had relied on the knowledge of the shaman to carry out the ceremony. Not only was he humble, but his knowledge of African culture and history was expansive, as he had shown in his little lesson. The elders realised how similar some of Aggrey's Fanti traditions were to their own and showed their new-found respect for him and the shaman by continuing to sit down in silence.

After some moments, Aggrey stood up and thanked the elders for making the events of the day possible. He told them that, just like his son Sandile, he was also a child of Cofimvaba and would be eternally linked to the spirit of the village of Cofimvaba. He thanked the shaman for leading the ceremony and then requested that they go and meet the women for lunch. The elders all concurred by nodding their heads in agreement, and the group made their way out of the kraal to meet with the women.

The elders, the shaman and Aggrey walked ahead, and Sandile and Anelisa followed behind the group. They walked to the front of the village church, where there was a small tent set up with a dining table for twenty-five people in the centre. This was enough to seat both the men and women. As the men approached, the women gathered around the table and waited for the elders of the village and Aggrey to take their seats.

Out of respect for the community, Sandile and Anelisa would be the last to take their seats at the table, after the women of the family. Although Sandile and Anelisa's seats were at the head of the table, they allowed their grandmother Rhundu and mother Phumla to take their seats and then they sat next to them with Aggrey. Mr. Mamphese, as the head of the village elders, was given the opportunity to pray for Anelisa and Sandile's union before they ate. He was not a man of many words and only had a few short words in prayer for Sandile and Anelisa.

"Dear Lord, bless the union of these two children of this village community. It must be understood by both of them that: 'if the neck is weak, the head shall wobble'! Let them understand that they both constitute the most important part of their support system, with help from their family and community, the community and family being the neck of their relationship. Amen."

After the prayer, they ate and reminisced and told stories of Sandile and Anelisa's childhood. Nobuhlali, being the record keeper of Sandile's life outside of the village, told stories of Sandile's growth in Sweden and how he had made the family proud by deciding to be circumcised at a young age in order to help his father protect the family. Nobuhlali spoke of Sandile's loyalty to the family as a loyal and obedient son to his mother and father. She spoke about how Sandile placed value on friendships and of the brotherly love he had developed with Simon and how they had supported one another through their childhood. She said she could not have asked the ancestors and God for a more loving brother than Sandile.

The community, especially Anelisa, sat intently and listened to Nobuhlali's stories of her brother. This was a way of getting to know Sandile again and welcome him and his family back to the community, as a son of the soil.

In returning the village of Cofimvaba, Sandile's family had a new-found appreciation for the values of ubuntu within their community. Aggrey and Phumla considered the sacrifices they had made for their family well worth the emotional and psychological pain they had endured during apartheid, both at home and on foreign lands.

Sandile also had a greater appreciation of what manhood meant within a community. He thought about the innocence of his childhood and how complex he had made manhood out to be. He was proud of himself that he had fulfilled his greatest ambition. He was no longer the immature young boy who had left Cofimvaba in a hurry to discover his manhood. He was now a self-assured young man who had rediscovered his culture, family and community.

Sandile closed his eyes and imagined all his aspirations being carried away by the African God Amun Rah to the ancestors and the heavens above. The ceremony of Sandile and Anelisa's rights of passage would be the final chapter marking the return of his family to the land of his birth and their home.

IN THE FOLLOWING years, Sandile would be the picture of health and happiness. Although he never got ill with bipolar again, he continued to take his medication for bipolar to assist with his moods, and to see his doctor Petra once a month for consultations. He also did not suffer from the visions he had had of his grandfather again. It seemed that, as soon as the shaman was done with the ceremony, his grandfather's spirit had left him in peace to live his life.

Over time, he and Anelisa, in building their family, became extremely religious. Out of respect for Jonas and as a testament to his memory, they decided to continue with his religion and became as devout Anglicans as Jonas had been. This was a faith to which they committed and which they would pass on to their children in memory of Jonas.

Every now and then, Sandile would consult his grandmother Rhundu, who had once practised as an inyanga. He had a fascination with all that was spiritual and sacred, and she guided him in his spiritual journey of spiritual self-discovery. She taught him about herbs and which herbs could assist his moods so that he could better manage his illness of bipolar. Over some years he stopped taking what he called white man's medicine and only took the herbs, as Rhundu had recommended. His moods became more stable, and he grew in his spirituality.

Life had taught Sandile and Anelisa the importance of family and community through prayer. Rhundu even went as far as telling Sandile her story with traditional medicine. According to Rhundu's story, she came from a long line of traditional healers. This to her might have explained why the shaman thought that Sandile should also become a practising shaman, because it was in his blood. Her father and her father's mother before him were inyangas and practised healing people with traditional herbs.

The apartheid government had banned her father and her father's mother from practising traditional medicine. This is because the apartheid government was of the opinion that it made people who consulted traditional healers ungovernable and nostalgic for an African past, which no longer existed. Over the years, traditional doctors were banned in urban South Africa by the apartheid government, because they did not have outcomes-based solutions and there were no documented case studies to show that traditional medicine worked.

Rhundu explained to Sandile that something was lost in African traditions in terms of exercising and maintaining the traditions because of the effects of apartheid and organised religion. She told him of how a lot of African tradition was watered down for the sake of modernity, in that they were seen as heretical by organised religion. Practising traditional doctors were no longer sticking to strict traditional practices and many of them had crossed over to witchcraft and other undesirable practices under the guise that they were traditional doctors.

She told him about the difficulty of practising authentic traditions in apartheid South Africa and that she could no longer manage to go against the status quo with a government that was in opposition to African culture. It was difficult for her to stop practising as an inyanga and opt for organised religion because she strongly felt that being an inyanga was her life's calling. Over the years, she had put all of the passion she had for being an inyanga into her religious practices and, although they left her fulfilled, there was still a void within her since she was not practising traditional medicine. Over the years she had practised in secret, helping members of the community where she could with traditional medicine.

Her story put into context her aspiration for Sandile and Nobuhlali to be grounded in African culture. He had a new-found understanding and love for his grandmother and the sacrifices that she had made during apartheid for her family.

As the years passed, Sandile and Nobuhlali also got to spend more time with Rhundu. They got to know her again both as a grandmother and a person with whom they could share their emotional and philosophical lives. She told them of her stories of perseverance and hope whilst they were out of the country and how difficult things had been for her. She told them it was faith in God and the ancestors that drove her belief that one day her family would be together again. She told them how the letters she had received from them over the years had made her proud of their growth and development as a young man and woman.

Their interest in the African continent had also consolidated her hopes that they would come back and contribute to the continent their learning as children of the soil. She concluded by telling them that their geographical distance from the continent had not deterred their ambition to have a spiritual proximity to the continent that reinforced their faith. Their lives had taken them to places far from home, their culture and way of life. But through it all they had endured, not only through their family, but also through their community. Life and apartheid had not robbed them of their dignity but had reinforced their faith.

For Aggrey and Phumla, work with their consulting company culminated in 1996, when they were invited to parliament to hear deputy president Thabo Mbeki's speech, *I am an African*. They were honoured for the work that they had done for the liberation movement in South Africa and abroad. Thabo Mbeki stood in front of parliament and delivered one of the most inspiring speeches of his career. South Africa was an infant democracy then. People were a combination of hopeful, proud and excited. The country was just an electrifying place to be. For them, the speech was the culmination of their work and sacrifices that they had made.

As they sat there at the event, they were taken back on the journey that their family had made. They were reminded of the open spirit of Sweden and the values of janteloven. As they sat in the gallery in parliament, they reminisced about the African spirit of Uhuru and South African values of ubuntu. These values had been entrenched within their family through tribulation, determination and faith. Thabo Mbeki's words echoed their greatest hopes on the continent whilst at the same time reinforcing their faith and determination of the people of the African continent. The words of the speech echoed their laments and joys of Africa.

"My mind and my knowledge of myself is formed by the victories that are the jewels in our African crown, the victories we earned from Isandhlawana to Khartoum, as Ethiopians and as the Ashanti of Ghana, as the Berbers of the desert.

I am the grandchild who lays fresh flowers on the Boer graves at St Helena and the Bahamas, who sees in the mind's eye and suffers the suffering of the simple peasant folk, death, concentration camps, destroyed homesteads, a dream in ruins.

I am the child of Nongqawuse. I am he who made it possible to trade in the world markets in diamonds, in gold, in the same food for which my stomach yearns.

I come from those who were transported from India and China, whose being resided in the fact, solely, that they were able to provide physical labour, who taught me that we could both be at home and be foreign, who taught me that human existence itself demanded that freedom was a necessary condition for that human existence.

Being part of all these people and in the knowledge that none dare contest that assertion, I shall claim that – I am an African."

Aggrey and Phumla's consulting firm over the following five years also prospered. They managed to sign on a lot of clients and still continued working on the NEPAD document with other African academics. The document that they spent so much of their lives working on was adopted at the 37th session of the Assembly of African Heads of State and Government in July 2001 in Lusaka, Zambia.

NEPAD's goals were threefold: to promote accelerated growth and sustainable development, to eradicate widespread and severe poverty, and to halt the marginalisation of Africa in the globalisation process. It was the culmination of their life's work and the sacrifices that they had made over the years with their family.

Aggrey's scenario work had added to the overall future forward looking orientation of the NEPAD document and the goals that it set for an African future, in attempting to recreate the African renaissance. Phumla's contribution had added to the idea that African wealth should not only be quantified in financial terms, but the value of the African people's indigenous and cultural capital should be taken into account when measuring the wealth of African nations. They had both been small participants with other African scholars and academics who had contributed to the document. It was the end of their lives as members of the diaspora and the beginning of their journey of the rediscovery of their love for the African continent.

Ten years after Sandile and Anelisa's rights of passage, Sandile received the honour of being the master of ceremonies at his sister's wedding to Simon in Nairobi. Just like Anelisa and Sandile, Nobuhlali and Simon did not have a white wedding. They had a small traditional ceremony, to which they invited their parents, some family and a small delegation from their communities. The event was small and intimate, with Rhundu leading the prayers for the event.

Nobuhlali and Simon had kept in contact with one another over the years, and, just like Sandile and Anelisa, their love for one another grew with distance. Shortly after she finished her university studies, Nobuhlali moved to Kenya to be closer to Simon. As always, she was very secretive about her and Simon's intentions and only gave her family sparse information about her feelings for him.

On rare occasions, she would tell the family that she hoped the war in Sundan with his father as the head of the liberation army would not damage Simon's soul, and then they had some indication of the depth of her feelings for him. It was only on the day she phoned her family in tears, saying that she was getting married to Simon, that they knew how much she loved and cared for him.

By the time they decided to marry, the Sudanese civil war had ended, having been one of the longest African conflicts in history from 1983 to 2005. It had been a war that had displaced millions of people with millions dead. Roughly two million people died as a result of war, famine and disease caused by the conflict. Four million people in southern Sudan were displaced. The civilian death toll was one of the highest of any war since World War II and was marked by a large number of human rights violations. These included slavery and mass killings. But through all the conflict, Simon's love for Nobuhlali blossomed. The war had not destroyed his soul.

His mother Faeema had moved back to Sudan shortly after the war to be with her husband Mr. Garang. Although war had torn her family apart and almost broken her spirit, and had came close to compromising her soul, her hopes for the future of Africa and her country were never more optimistic. Her love for her husband had brought her comfort in difficult times. Simon had stayed behind in Kenya, as it had become his home over the years and his roots were now firmly settled in Nairobi.

Sandile and Anelisa had one child named Jonas, whose godfather was Simon. Sandile had a thriving psychology practice and Anelisa started her own law firm. As per the African shaman's words, they were blessed in life and in their work. Although Sandile thought about what it would be like to be a practising shaman every now and then, he would not have replaced his family for anything. He was content with his life and the decision he had made during his rights of passage ceremony.

Time had not separated a friendship between Simon and Sandile that had been forged in difficult times. Time had also not separated a love between Nobuhlali and Simon that had been nurtured in their aspiration to be conscious young Africans on a foreign land. Their time growing up in Sweden and Kenya had awoken a longing in Nobuhlali to fully express her womanhood through the love she had for Simon.

At his sister's wedding, Sandile spoke of the law of Jante in that we all come into this world as equals and we leave as equals in death. He spoke of the kindness of strangers when he had to flee South Africa on a day's notice. He spoke about developing trust in the kindness of others in difficult times. He spoke of the enduring spirit of Uhuru and ubuntu, which had been the basis for their rediscovery of African cultural beauty.

He spoke about the common bonds of humanity that unite us all, and that at times faith might waiver but the enduring human spirit always prevails. He spoke about the ancestors and their guidance in this world and asked Nobuhlali and Simon to nurture their faith in love under a forgiving and loving God. He spoke about the bonds of a friendship, which over the years had become the basis for Simon and Nobuhlali's love for one another. He spoke about Simon being the brother he'd never had and how the ancestors and the universe had conspired to bring their paths together to learn and love together.

He concluded by using the example of his grandmother, of faith and fortitude through tribulation, and requested that Nobuhlali persevere through good and troublesome times as his grandmother had done during apartheid. She had maintained faith that one day she would be united with her family and never gave up hope in the idea of them being together one day.

It was his hope that Nobuhlali would foster a sense of hope and be guided by a principled and pragmatic spirit within her relationship as their mother Phumla had been in their childhood with her father. He reaffirmed his faith in family and community and reassured Nobuhlali and Simon that there is beauty in love.

9

A month after Nobuhlali's wedding, Rhundu passed away. The family over the last ten years had spent enough time with her not to feel like her passing was robbing the family of time missed. Over the years, she had spent time getting to know Sandile and Nobuhlali again. She had participated in both their weddings as the most special moments in their lives. She was alive to witness the culmination of Aggrey and Phumla's work and the consolidation of their sacrifices.

Although she was the foundation of the family, they felt that, like Jonas, she had made her contribution and it was now time for her to rest.

Her service was a conservative Methodist funeral. The entire village of Cofimvaba showed up to send her off. There were many impromptu speeches with numerous people from the village wanting to get a moment to share how Rhundu had touched their lives. The event was a solemn affair filled with love, affinity and wonderful memories of Rhundu being shared by the community.

When the funeral was over, Sandile walked five minutes to the local park where he used to look for cow dung as a child. He walked to the park on his own, trying to gather his thoughts. He could smell the cow dung mixed with a scent of grass that the cows were grazing on. He was reminded of his childhood. He was reminded of the safety of his village and his innocence about life. He was reminded of the times when he was a little boy and the centre of his life was Anelisa. He thought about his grandmother's well-told religious stories and how they had fuelled his imagination. He remembered telling them to Anelisa with such enthusiasm, as if it were the first time he had heard them.

He thought about all those moments spent in the anticipation of manhood and wishing never to be called inkwenkwe again. He had now reached manhood and the ideas of legacy were starting to settle in his mind. What would he pass on to his child? What values would he have to entrench in his family to ensure that his grandmother's memory and legacy were preserved? Her ideas of her interpretation of Uhuru and the foundations of ubuntu with her community flooded his mind.

With the death of Rhundu, Sandile would have no reason in the future to come back to the village of Cofimvaba. However, he would take the values of family and community with him, no matter where he went. They were entrenched in his soul through tribulation, faith and love. Cofimvaba had birthed a boy – inkwenkwe – but had raised a man.